Totally Bound Publishing books by CC Dragon

Southern Belle Cozy Mysteries
The Mint Julep Murder

I0570502

Southern Belle Cozy Mysteries

THE MINT JULEP MURDER

CC DRAGON

The Mint Julep Murder
ISBN # 978-1-83943-888-2
©Copyright CC Dragon 2020
Cover Art by Louisa Maggio ©Copyright June 2020
Interior text design by Claire Siemaszkiewicz
Totally Bound Publishing

THE MINT
JULEP MURDER

Chapter One

I really need to powder my nose!

Gran had taught me that that was how polite women referred to needing to use the ladies' room. I was only ten minutes from my ultimate destination—I could make it. Hideous traffic had already made me late, but this close to midnight, nothing was open in the tiny town of Sweet Grove, so there were no options anyway.

I should've gone when I stopped back in Nashville to gas up my baby, an old white pickup truck that had never failed me. I could deal with a gross gas station bathroom—I always had hand sanitizer.

Unfortunately, there had been too many truckers and sketchy wannabe musicians at the gas station. I'd paid at the pump and whipped out of there before any of them had wandered over to creep on me. Good old southern boys just out to help were now often hard to distinguish from the creepy men looking to throw a pretty girl into their trunk so they could do terrible things later.

Not that I was much to look at, but some guys saw a petite blonde alone and thought I was easy. Usually those were the wrong kind of guys — generally the drunk sort. Better safe than sorry. I didn't want to end up in someone's basement being a story on the news. Gran would worry. She was probably already worried.

Moving back to my hometown hadn't been the plan, but the plan had changed. At least I'd be safe — no one locked their doors and everyone knew everyone. Not that everyone liked everyone — there were subgroups. The quilting ladies, the charity and church group, the old guys sitting outside the bait and hunting shop, and so on. The farmers were a tight-knit bunch. There wasn't much industry around except for the distillery that was between our town and the next. It was a huge employer and sat on unincorporated land.

I glanced up at the mountains that were pitch black now. All my life, I'd been warned about going up in the hills. The true hillbillies lived up there. They worked when they wanted to, and if they shot a deer, they'd quit because they had food enough for a while. Mainly it was subsistence farming and scavenging — a very simple life. They didn't like outsiders. When I'd been little, there'd been stories about pipe-smoking grannies who'd whip out a double-barreled shotgun on anyone who got close to their property. Back then, they were making moonshine.

Today it was far more likely that they were growing weed in the thick forest areas. Maybe running stills too, but the marijuana was lucrative and hard for the police to find. Part of me wondered how they sold it or even moved it from way up in the mountains, but it wasn't my business. I preferred legal work and not needing guns to keep my business safe.

Still, Sweet Grove wasn't perfect. There were gossips and judgmental people who made everyone's business their own business. One Sweet Grove resident always tried to get the town to go dry—every year it was a petition or they ran for mayor.

I drove by the Town Hall and the community center. The paired buildings were quaint but very official looking. The whole town was respectable, but some of the places were on the fringe. My friend's bar was on the outskirts, but always full, and the mechanic shop had a used car lot next to it that people said was sketchy—probably a few stray dogs, and teens looking to buy some cigarettes or beer.

Back home, I needed to be on my best behavior. In Atlanta, most people had good southern manners, except tourists of course, but in the city, people generally minded their own business. The judgmental types weren't nearly as noticeable or concentrated as in a small town where secrets were harder to keep, and everyone knew everyone and their great-grandparents back to the Civil War.

I visited every month to check on Gran, so Sweet Grove didn't feel completely foreign. Normally I managed to pop in mid-week on a day off. It was only a three-hour drive, more or less, so I was back for work the next day. That way I'd usually avoided running into too many blasts from the past at home, but could check on Gran's bills, pills and anything else that came up.

It wasn't enough anymore. Gran needed more help and support than a weekly check-in.

There was no one on the street so I put my foot down to get through town and to Gran's big, old, sprawling ranch home faster. Grandpa had believed in brick houses, Chevy trucks, Jack Daniel's whiskey, yellow labs and that there was no such thing as too much barbecue.

He didn't believe in seeing the doc, either, so he'd died when I was little of a massive heart attack. The docs had said he must've had smaller ones, but he'd powered through.

I barely remembered him, but Gran talked about him so much that his philosophies were like Bible stories to me. He never wanted a two-story house because his great-grandmother had lost a toddler to a nasty fall down a long flight of stairs. If that wasn't proof that people in small towns had really long memories, it was proof of something. Superstition maybe.

I slowed down for a stop sign, but there was literally no one on the road. Main Street had a variety of old buildings, with every business someone could need. A couple of restaurants, Gran's shop, a lawyer, an insurance agent, the bank and, farther down, the florist and grocery store. I'd already passed by the red brick schools lined up from elementary to middle to high school. Across from the schools was the simple white siding church with the community center connected.

I could drive these streets with my eyes closed with the complete lack of traffic. Rolling along, I was almost through the main part of town and headed for the far end. *So close.*

Red and blue lights caught my eye in the rearview mirror.

"Oh, crap," I said.

Pulling my truck over, I felt like an idiot. I shifted to Park and grabbed my license from my purse. Looking back, I saw it was Sheriff Monroe. What was he doing out in the middle of the night patrolling?

The potbellied old grump moseyed out of his police SUV and up to my window. He put on his hat and adjusted it like he was a supermodel on a catwalk.

I rolled down the window and handed him my license and registration. "Hi, Sheriff."

"Annabelle Baxter? Where's the fire?" He chuckled and shone the flashlight on me.

I smiled. "I just wanted to get home. Traffic was awful around Nashville and I want to check on Gran. I'm really late."

"Late isn't enough of an excuse to go flying through town and endangering people," he said.

I looked around. "What people?"

"Don't you sass me, Belle. Laws are there for a reason."

"I know, I'm sorry. If I had my druthers, I'd have been home hours ago. I'm moving back and I didn't want Gran to worry," I explained. I could hear Gran now... *Being good is doing what's right when no one is looking.* I'd botched today nicely.

He huffed a big exhale of air. "Moving back? I thought you went off to college."

"I did. Hospitality management. I graduated and have been working," I said.

"Hospitality? That should be something a good southern girl knows without schooling. But given your family, it couldn't hurt. Did you ever find your mama?" he asked.

My face burned. "No. I was working and going to school. It wasn't about her. I reckon Gran needs more help now."

"She sure does. Nearly burned down her kitchen last month." He shifted his hat.

"Bless her heart. It won't happen again. It was an accident. Her old dog had passed and someone gave her a new puppy who'd jumped up for something while she was cooking. I told her to crate the puppy, but she thought that was mean. She was so busy trying to save the puppy from eating something it shouldn't that the fire got out of hand." I rambled through what he already probably had been briefed on.

"I know it. We were all there for her. She's fixin' to turn seventy, rumor has it. Ladies don't like talking about their real age, but I commend you for stepping up and looking after her. That mother of yours is nowhere to be found." The sheriff looked at the book in his hand.

"Thanks. I'm here and I'll handle things. Find a job and get settled. No more late-night driving or speeding at any time of day. I really do appreciate ya being there for Gran," I promised.

"We don't have a Starbucks for you to work at," he teased.

I resisted rolling my eyes. "Well, it helped with tuition, room and board for college. I'm not too big for my britches to work where I can get it."

"Fancy drinks—people here can make their own coffee. You'll have your hands full with that shop of your Gran's too. She's a charitable woman, but you have to draw a line between charity and business."

"Yes, sir." That had me more worried.

Something started ringing and I knew by the tune that it wasn't my phone.

"I'll let you off with a warning this time, but you slow it way down. Fast girls aren't what men really want. None of us want to see you turn out like your momma." He wagged a finger at me.

I bit my tongue and nodded. "Yes, sir. Thank you. I'm glad to be on old stomping grounds."

As he walked away, I started to roll up my window. I heard him mutter something like, "Back like a bad penny."

One would think that in modern times, people wouldn't be quite so spiteful and judgy. Widows with kids got full proper respect and admiration. Single moms with an ex but not a dead husband garnered some respect along with a "Bless her heart" sympathy. Her man didn't stick around but she'd been married and was doing right by her kids—good old southern folks could respect the effort.

But when the dad was way gone before the kid was born and the mom bailed as soon as she got sprung from the hospital, people started to worry the kid was a bad seed or something.

That was me.

Everyone in town knew my little history. Some pitied me while others judged my parents hard and assumed I'd turn out just like them. I felt worse for Gran. She'd lost a daughter and gotten stuck with me. If she hadn't claimed me, I'd have ended up a ward of the state. There were no aunts or uncles or extended family to lean on.

I pulled back onto the road, into the non-existent traffic. Part of me wished Sweet Grove had a Starbucks. I'd be running it in a few months and that'd be good money. I'd left a great job in Atlanta for extremely limited prospects here.

But bringing Gran to Atlanta, away from everyone she knew and to a big city that was confusing—that wasn't an option. Well, it was the last resort. This was for family. I had to do the right thing. I'd made my mistakes growing up, but I'd die before I turned into my mother and walked away. Sweet Grove wasn't perfect, but it was home.

The pale-yellow brick of Gran's ranch house triggered a million memories of my childhood, but I was so frustrated and tired I couldn't even get emotional. I parked my baby in the driveway, grabbed my overnight duffel filled with essentials and tried the back door. Gran had left it unlocked. Most people only locked their houses at night, if at all. I'd grab the big suitcases tomorrow and really unpack once I'd slept.

The sharp bark of the puppy made me jump. I missed old Reg, a sweet and calm dog. *Puppyhood won't last forever*, I reminded myself, and the new dog was cute.

After locking the door behind me, I slipped into the washroom off the laundry room, all very near the backdoor. Gran called it the servant's bath. Not that we'd ever had any servants, but it was a basic square shower and toilet with a sink. Nothing frilly or decorated like the guest bath up front or her master bath.

I relieved myself and heard the barking growing louder. Quickly I washed my hands and opened the door.

"Get out! I'm calling nine-one-one!" Gran yelled.

The double-barreled shotgun pointed at me made me very grateful I'd gotten to the bathroom before she'd made it out of bed, or I'd have wet the floor!

"Gran, it's me!" I shouted.

She looked quite dangerous, all of five feet tall with long gray hair and her old orange robe cinched at her waist. Her slippers showed her pride in the Tennessee Volunteers, but it looked like the puppy had been chewing them up a bit. Her usually sweet face finally registered what I'd said and went from serious to shocked.

"Belle? What are you doing here?" She lowered the gun then hugged it to her body.

"You knew I was coming home. I got stuck in traffic. I called, but you didn't answer." I gently took the gun from her, and I could breathe again.

"I fell asleep waiting for you and I thought… I'm sorry, I forgot. I thought you were an intruder. Sorry, darlin'," she said.

"It's okay, but I'll keep the gun in my room now." I looked down at the puppy bouncing for attention. "Have you named it?"

"Duke, and it's a he. At least until we get him snipped," she said proudly.

"Definitely snipped as soon as possible. Duke. Well, he made a puddle on the floor, careful not to step in it." I snapped on the light. "Go to bed and I'll get this cleaned up."

"No, it's my dog. I'll clean it up. You go get some sleep. But first, admire my newly remodeled kitchen." She grabbed a mop from the mud room.

The kitchen was now the fanciest room in the house, with stone counter tops and a new stove with a lot more buttons. Plus, a new fridge, microwave and a new kitchen table. The colors were apple red and a cream that looked lovely, but none of it hinted at a bargain.

"Gran, did the insurance pay for all this?" I asked.

"No, but there was smoke damage and the appliances were getting old anyway. I got a little equity line of credit from the bank. I got a better deal when I bought all new appliances from the store together in a bundle. New washer and dryer in the mud room too," she explained.

I shook my head. "You said the business wasn't turning a big profit right now," I said.

"I know. I'm not senile. This is my home. I need to be able to cook and wash my clothes. While I was having things repaired, it seemed like the best time to replace what needed replacing. We'll talk about the business tomorrow." She yawned and put the mop back.

"Okay. I'm going to try to get some sleep." I hugged her and the familiar smell finally signaled that I was truly home.

"Night, dear. I'll bring Duke into my room so he won't bug you." Gran patted her thigh and the dog followed.

"Good night." Once I heard her door click shut, I set the gun down carefully then slung the strap for my duffel over my shoulder. Thinking ahead, I poured myself a glass of water, flipped off the light and picked up the gun with my free hand.

I closed the door to my room and locked it. Carrying a loaded gun when tired should be illegal. I put the water down on the nightstand then tucked the gun under my bed. Finally, I dropped the duffel on my bed.

"Darn, my purse!" I went back out to my truck and grabbed my purse from the front seat.

I slammed the door to my truck louder than I meant to. Luckily, we had a few acres of land so the neighbors wouldn't be bothered. I made sure my doors were locked and headed into the house, locking the doors behind me. Atlanta living had made me a compulsive door locker.

Back in my room, I felt twelve again. Not much had changed. I had an old guitar hanging on the wall for decoration. My old keyboard sat on the desk. The queen-sized bed had a wrought-iron secondhand frame and a gently used mattress from an estate sale.

We'd never been made of money. I wanted to strangle whoever had talked Gran into those expensive appliances. Sure, they may have been due for replacing, but high-end fancy was more than she needed. I wanted her to have the best of everything, but no job I could get in Sweet Grove would provide that sort of income. That was why I'd stayed in Atlanta after college, so I could work my way up and send her money.

I had some college loans to pay back too, but I'd been frugal and made use of every scholarship and program I could. Gran would insist the house and her preserves shop weren't my problem, but who else was there?

No one.

I fought off tears and changed from my boot-cut jeans, gym shoes and T-shirt norm into a sleep shirt advertising my alma mater. After unpacking a few basic outfits and my makeup bag, I used a wipe to remove my makeup. It was a delicate thing—Gran never wanted me made up like one of those pageant girls, but going out with nothing was practically as bad.

I'd found a good balance. Hospitality required a good face without looking too flashy.

Pushing back the peach quilt, I noticed my nails needed a fresh painting. But should I bother? Here, I wasn't around clients like in a fancy hotel. What really mattered now? I wasn't sure—except for Gran, of course. I had a few friends I was eager to see and plenty of others, like the sheriff, who I was fine not running into.

My head hit the pillow and I said my prayers. Grateful for not getting a ticket and not getting shot. Sorry for all the awful things I felt about the people who'd swindled my gran with that kitchen. I'd fix it all the best I could, but the worst was yet to come.

The business was a cute little preserves shop with fresh baked goods that varied by Gran's mood. People popped in and ordered preserves, but most swung by for breakfast treats. It'd been a nice notion when my grandpa was alive and had made good money as a plumber. He could fix just about anything. When he'd died, the insurance had covered what was owed on the house and the cars plus funeral expenses. Gran had widow's social security, a little pension and zero debt until this lovely credit line fiasco.

Was the business helping or hurting Gran's overall finances? That was the question.

Then again, life wasn't only about money. Was my presence here just another reminder for Gran of my mom who'd bailed—no cards or calls in over twenty years—who should be here taking care of her mother? I didn't want Gran suffering from having to protect or defend me—I could take care of myself, but the roles had to be different this time. I was here to take care of her—whether she liked it or not.

Chapter Two

Duke barking and scratching at my door woke me a couple of times, but I was tired enough to roll over and go back to sleep until nine. Clearly, Gran hadn't managed to keep him in her room all night.

It wasn't my habit to sleep in, but nothing about yesterday had been normal. I'd needed a decent night's sleep to face the day ahead.

I shuffled into the kitchen, expecting a puppy nipping at my ankles, but apparently Gran had put in a dog run and Duke was outside enjoying the good weather, bird sightings and exercise.

Once I'd gotten coffee in my system, I found a note on the kitchen table.

Belle, went to the shop. Breakfast is the busiest time – people drop in before work. Come by for breakfast and we can talk about the shop. Or you can just say hi to everyone! Love, Gran

After a shower and careful hair styling and makeup, I put my suitcases in the house. I checked that the dog had a huge bowl of water and a backup bowl in case he tipped one over. The weather wasn't going to be too hot today, plus part of the run was covered to give him shade, and I figured he'd be happier outside than in.

Less destructive at least.

In my big suitcase, I found an old messenger bag and loaded it with my tablet, my dainty purse, a refillable water bottle, a notebook and pen and my phone charger. I slung the bag across my body and tucked my phone into my pocket.

The drive into town was quick, but the streets were busy now. Lots of cars and people all over — nothing like Atlanta, but that was a nice change. I parked around back by Gran's little sedan and went in through the door marked for deliveries.

The kitchen was only partially used in the old bakery. She did preserves in big batches based on peak fruit harvests but the baking she did at home and brought in. I wasn't great at canning or baking, but Gran had made sure I could cook well enough.

My dream was to open a B&B around here for tourists visiting Nashville who wanted a small-town-feel option. The city could be crazy, expensive and dangerous in some areas. My place could offer day trips to the city with plans for food, things to see and all designed for the people's interests. Kids or no kids? Music or history?

That was just a dream. For now, I had to handle what was in front of me. I found the office and flipped through the stacks of receipts and monthly statements. Gran used a basic system and had someone do her taxes. She printed out everything monthly in case something crashed so I didn't even need to snoop for a password.

The numbers weren't terrible, but the profit was slim after expenses. Frankly, I was shocked she was turning a profit. Odds were good that she wasn't reporting all her expenses.

I went back to the summer last year and a few months were in the red. Hospitality might not seem like a normal college degree for some, but we did cover a lot of business classes that I really valued now.

My stomach declared that breakfast was late and I headed to the front. The space behind the counter was nicely laid out. The preserves were shelved on distressed wooden racks on one side of the dining area. There were only five round tables with four chairs at each. The strawberry and blueberry tones trimmed the oak shelves and counter. It was a pretty shop with big windows that faced Main Street.

Opposite the shelves was a big old coffee maker with two pots full and to-go cups, sugar and creamers. A little sign proclaimed *Free Coffee For All Customers.*

Gran was living in another era.

The counter next to the preserves had biscuits in a warmer along with some homemade muffins. Another little sign offered a breakfast special of two biscuits with preserves for two dollars. Not outrageous, but add in the free coffee and she was shortchanging herself big time.

"Belle, finally. Did you sleep well?" Gran asked.

She was sitting at one of the tables with four old men.

"Yes, I just had to catch up and take in my suitcases. It's sort of quiet here," I said.

"You missed the rush when everyone is off to work and school. It'll be a trickle of people at most for the rest of the day. Some kids come in after school, but it's a morning rush. Like a bakery," she said.

Like a bakery, maybe we should stock more baked goods? Have order forms so people could order ahead for meetings, weekends in, or whatever? I kept my thoughts to myself for now. Changing everything all at once would only upset Gran.

She turned to her admirers. "This is Freddie, Joe, Milan and Abe. They like to hang out here and keep me company."

"Nice to meet you. Retirement has its advantages," I said.

"And its disadvantages. If you earn too much money, they cut your social security." Freddie shook his head. "You should know that, if you're here to help with the business."

"I see. Is that why you give the coffee away, Gran?" I asked.

"Get yourself some biscuits and eat. You're always crabby when you're hungry," Gran said.

"We don't just take up space. If more people come in, we give up the table. We make sure no one runs off with a jar and doesn't pay or no one takes coffee for free without a purchase." Abe tipped his baseball cap.

"How kind." I dished up two biscuits and slathered on strawberry preserves, then sat at one of the stools along the wall and the counter that ran around the seating area. That layout maximized how many people we could seat, but we weren't filling it. That was as good as it could be.

"The boys also help me when I do fairs and such around the county. Help me carry things and set up tables and talk me up," Gran said.

"That's very nice of them." I got myself some coffee.

"Are you going to work here with your Gran?" Joe asked.

"Of course she's here to help me, but I don't need a babysitter. I told her she could keep her fancy job in Atlanta. One little fire doesn't mean I need a keeper," she said.

"We helped clean all that out too," Milan bragged and tugged on his brown suspenders.

"Aren't you a peach? But there's a lot to consider. This earnings cap for social security. The line of credit to remodel the kitchen at home. I'm not sure what I'm going to do, but I can help here until I figure it out. I have to get up to speed." I saw so much room for expansion and improvement.

"Too bad there's no Starbucks for you to work at. Or a hotel," Freddie teased.

"That's a shame. People love fancy coffee," I replied.

"The young people come in sometimes and want funny coffee drinks. And smoothies too. And tea." Gran chuckled.

"At a preserves shop? They can get that stuff a couple towns over. Coffee shop or something. Ridiculous prices," Milan commented.

I studied the space. There was plenty of room behind the counter for a big coffee machine and blenders. We already had the fruit connections, but smaller buys for daily smoothies could work. Flavorings for coffees, vitamins shots as well. It would just expand things. Chai and other teas would be good too.

Smiling, I let the older generation debate what coffee should be. Gran was a purist about black coffee, nothing added. Most of her men liked at least a little sugar.

Thankfully, the bell over the door rang, and it was Katie!

"Thank God you're back!" Katie ran over and hugged me.

I hugged her and refused to cry. "I'm so glad you never left. You're a sight for sore eyes!"

We started talking at the same time as if we were teenagers again.

"Why don't you two take your breakfast in the back and chat? We can't hear ourselves talk," Gran suggested.

I refilled my coffee and got one for Katie.

I hadn't had a lot of friends growing up. My mom's reputation, coupled with her running off and leaving after she had me, had left a mark. Most of the kids I'd gone to school with had been steered away from me by their parents. Small towns had long memories.

Katie's mom was around but had been married and divorced multiple times, so we were sort of the kids from *those* types of families. She hadn't changed a bit. Long brown curly hair, slim and tall. Full-on cowgirl with boots, jeans with a shiny belt buckle, tank top that advertised her bar and funky western jewelry.

"So, how are things?" she asked.

I shrugged. "The business is barely turning a profit. Gran redid the kitchen at home with all pricy stuff."

"I saw that. She was determined to buy quality." Kate rolled her eyes.

"It is, but you can buy a quality brand without all the fancy upgrades. That's done and all I can do is see about the line of credit and those terms. Here, I think we need to make more money. Coffee options and smoothies are a good start, and people are asking for them, but..." I trailed off.

"But?" Katie prompted. "People are dying for fancy coffee and teas. It's like micro-brews and stuff. At first no one admits they want something other than good old American-brand mass-produced beers, but once they try it…"

Katie owned the Honey Buckle, a bar on the edge of town. There was live music and fun! Her dad had passed suddenly not long after we'd graduated high school and his life insurance had all been paid out to her, so she'd put it into something she loved – entertaining.

Talk about judgment, a single woman owning a bar…but she'd proven herself. She'd worked hard and people in town had to admit that at least her father had acknowledged her, even if her parents hadn't stayed married. Her daddy had provided for her and she hadn't blown it on anything stupid. She had a thriving business.

"You'd know about the town and what sells. I just have to sell Gran on it. Plus, figure out the social security thing," I said.

Katie frowned. "What about it?"

"There are earnings caps, I guess," I said.

Katie waved her hand. "For your gran. You can retitle it into your name or joint ownership. Change things. If the business is in only your name, you can make all the money you want and take care of Gran. Just pay her a salary just short of what would start to erode her benefits. Sad that people have to play games to get what they paid into the social security system and to make a little more so they can have a decent life. It's not like it's a gift from the government."

"I know, but that's not the worst part. She might not want to give up ownership," I said.

Katie sipped her coffee. "One thing at a time. You turn this place around and get it to bring in big money, then show her how she can keep her checks. I mean, she paid into the system and so did your grandpa, and you can make the business mega profitable. Win-win."

"I could pay off the bank line she took out. They don't care where the money comes from. But I'll need supplies, machines, and it's not cheap to do it right," I said.

"It never is. You have to have the vision and believe in yourself. The first year I had the Honey Buckle, I barely hung on. But the right music, the right beer options and the right feel and people showed up. They keep showing up. You can make that here too. Coffee is far more socially acceptable than beer," Katie reminded me.

I smiled. "It's just not my business. I have to convince Gran. But what else do I have to do? I don't know of any jobs around here. Not making what I need with skills that I have."

"Well, you can always pick up some shifts at the bar. Waitressing you can do and I can show you the ropes of bartending," she offered.

"Thanks, and if you need me, I'm there. I won't take the work from someone else, though. I need to focus on the problems at hand," I admitted.

"You get the equipment and supplies. You get a new menu, charge for coffee and all that. Up the prices to something normal — not Atlanta, but reasonable. Do a one-per-person free fancy coffee drink promotion — print up coupons or something. Have some non-coffee frozen drinks so kids can have them too. Oh, make up signature drinks based on your customers. Have a big grand reopening day. I'll help. I can get some of the girls who waitress to pitch in too. The bar can't be open at seven a.m. Not in this county." Kate flashed a big smile.

"Thank you!" I hugged her.

"What else is wrong?" she asked with the instincts only a best friend for decades would possess.

I released her and focused on my food. "Sheriff pulled me over last night. I was going too fast, but no one was out. I had to pee. I was late and worried about Gran. It'll be all over town later today."

"It already is, but who cares? He let you off with a warning," Katie said.

"Back again and already in trouble. Already getting pity." I sighed.

Katie sighed heavily. "Stop listening to what people say. It was childish crap when we were kids and the parents...they were jealous of our moms. My mom didn't stay in a bad marriage. Granted, she got married six times and never seemed to get it right, but she didn't stay and let herself or her kids get abused or poorly treated. She believed she deserved better."

"Brave. Nothing wrong with being single," I said.

"True. Your mom followed her dreams. She'll be back someday." Katie nodded.

What were best friends for? She'd been saying that since we were six years old. Twenty-one years later, she couldn't really back off on it now. Rumor around town was that my mom had had a dream of making it in the music business and hadn't wanted to be tied down by a kid.

"That doesn't matter anymore. I have to make sure Gran is okay. She took care of me when it wasn't her job. I have to make sure she's safe." I envied that Katie knew who her dad was, even if he hadn't been in her life too much. He'd left her his life insurance and she'd met him before he'd passed.

I could sulk about my parents all day, but I never let myself. I shoved it away and focused on what I could do. Gran had a good space and some loyal customers. We could grow that without alienating her base.

"You'll take great care of her. I just don't want you to get stuck in what people thought of your mom or how your gran does things. You're not retirement age. Change is part of life and you have good ideas. You don't have to settle for what people give you or the hand you get dealt. You're better than that," Katie said.

"You can think that, but we both know people judge. Remember the Andersons? Their son was cooking meth and blew up their trailer? The whole family moved to the west end of the state and put the boy in rehab. People still talk about the trailer-trash family with the meth-cooker kid," I reminded her.

"They raised a meth head. You did nothing wrong. Your gran did nothing wrong. Don't let them make you feel second-class. Annabelle, I'm serious, don't get sucked into the senior center or geriatric set because you're doing right by Gran. You're still young." Katie was always good for a pep talk.

"Thanks." I took a deep breath. "If you need help at the bar, I'm there. It'll be the best excuse to get me around young people. If it's to help you, Gran won't mind a bit."

"No help needed right now, but come by tonight and have a little fun. Call it training for busier times. I need your opinion on a new band I've been letting play. I love music but have no talent for picking it. I enjoy it all. You've got the best taste and some skill." Katie took a long drink of her coffee.

"Good girls play piano," I repeated one of Gran's many mottos. She'd done her level best to mold me into a proper southern lady so I'd be less likely to get criticized and belittled for my mother's bad choices. I couldn't help that I had a little talent and a lot of love for music.

When I'd gone off to college, there'd been bets that I'd never come back, like my mom. That or I'd fail in the music scene and return hooked on drugs or pregnant, possibly both. I'd beaten the odds so far.

"I can't play a tambourine. Drinks are on the house," Katie offered.

I shook my head. "You don't need to do that. I'll be there for the music and friends."

"Good. You look like you need a little fun." Katie stood up. "You have room to store things back here. If you find a good gently used coffee machine and start with some supplies...see what takes off. You can expand slowly. It's stressful at times, but you'll always be tinkering and refining as trends change. That's the business," she said.

"You're right. I think of Sweet Grove as never changing, but with the Internet and a million TV channels streaming on phones and all that, we're not cut off. People here want to try new things and be trendy," I said. "I can do this."

"Good. I have to go do some inventory. See you later." She gave me a quick hug. "I'll sneak out the back. Your gran's group of men always has to chat."

I couldn't argue with that logic and went out the front with my coffee cup.

"Where's Katie?" Gran asked.

"She went out the back. I guess she has to do inventory today. We'll catch up more later." I refilled my coffee and found myself agreeing that tea would be a good option. There was a pot of decaf, but some flavor options wouldn't be too radical. Heck, the gas stations around here probably had that.

"She's planning something. I can see the smoke coming out of her ears," Joe chuckled.

The bell rang and we all turned.

"Good morning, Pastor," Gran said.

The man was young for a pastor, thirty at the oldest. Not bad-looking at all. He had light brown hair, blue eyes, a lean build and a calm demeanor.

"Good morning, Mrs. Baxter. I heard you had an addition to your family." The pastor looked at me.

"Oh yes. Belle, this is Pastor Luke Nelson. Pastor, my granddaughter, Belle Baxter. She's back. She went to Atlanta for college and worked to build up her experience. Now she's joining the family business." Gran beamed.

I held out my hand. "Pleased to meet you, Pastor."

"Very nice to meet you. I'm sure I'll see you Sunday with your grandmother." He held my hand tight and it felt very genuine.

Gran jumped in before I could answer. "Actually, I was thinking about that. You said last Sunday that you need someone to play the piano for the choir. Belle is a great piano player."

"Really?" The pastor smiled at me.

"I can play piano. I'm probably a little rusty. I didn't even have room for my keyboard in Atlanta. I practiced a bit when I could," I admitted.

"Why don't you drop by choir practice tomorrow afternoon and we'll give you a try? Music is always pleasing, and the more the merrier," the pastor said. "Three o'clock at the church."

"Sure, I'll see you then." I couldn't say no. I loved playing music and helping out wasn't the problem. Being on display for the town to see and judge? That made me a bit queasy.

Chapter Three

Good girls go to church, not bars...

Gran's words nagged at me while I parked at the Honey Buckle. I'd had to remind her that Katie owned the bar and had plenty of bouncers. Katie had three half-brothers from her mother's subsequent marriages and they were all football players who didn't let anyone mess with their sis or her business. People called them Huey, Dewy and Lewy, but they were Harry, Dave and Lucas.

I'd remembered to put on some dangly silver earrings and a charm bracelet a boyfriend from college had given me. The extra feminine touches kept Gran from fussing about one more thing.

Walking into the bar, I waved at the familiar faces. A few returned the greeting, but some looked me up and down and glanced away. Cattiness didn't end in high school.

The Honey Buckle was huge. Tons of tables filled the space to the walls, except for a large stage for live bands, and the jukebox in the corner. The bar section was toward the back with a hall beyond that most people never noticed, where they had a small kitchen and restrooms. The round bar had the usual stools all done in cherry wood. Above the bar and around on the walls were guitars and posters for rock and country music performers. The place served young and old, as long as they had ID, and it was *the* best spot to have fun in Sweet Grove.

I headed for the bar and found Katie serving up beer and enjoying herself. She had her hair up in a ponytail with a black cowboy hat cocked on her head, matching the black T-shirt she wore that displayed the bar logo.

Hopping onto a free bar stool, I checked out the specials.

"Hey, you actually came out. Good!" Katie said with a bit more surprise than I'd expected.

"You thought I wouldn't?" I asked.

"You had a long first day. I'd have given you a pass tonight to catch up on sleep," Katie said.

"Longer than you know. The pastor came in and Gran suggested I play piano for the choir or whatever." I sighed.

"You love the piano," Katie said.

I checked out all the stuff she had behind the bar. "I do, and I'm happy to help, but I need to focus on the business. I came up with a short list of new additions I can offer with minimal supplies."

"Cool. You better charge for them," Katie said.

"I will, and regular or decaf coffee will be one dollar with any purchase or three dollars without purchase, no more freebies," I said.

"Good. The travel cups are a good size, so it's fair. Free refills?"

"On regular coffee? Naturally, I'm not a monster. I can't let people take advantage of Gran, but if they stick around and buy more stuff, free coffee is fine. A fancy coffee machine is expensive, but I can do some smoothies to start," I replied.

"We have an extra blender, if you want to borrow it. Most people don't want foo-foo drinks. But you'll have to lend it to me for Cinco de Mayo. Margaritas are a big seller then," Katie offered.

"You're the best! I'm going to have to run into Nashville to get some cups, straws, coffee flavors and teas. At the least, I'll splurge on an extra coffee maker for now, a smaller one for the decaf. There aren't a huge number of decaf drinkers, but Gran has those big industrial coffee makers. Love them, but that's a lot of decaf," I said.

"You're always thinking, Belle. If there's anything I can help with, let me know. But some cold brew pitchers and stuff can't be too bad. My distributors don't sell coffee and such, but napkins and stirrers I can front you," she offered.

I hugged her over the bar. "Thanks, but I don't want you supplying me. I can do this. I saved up some money working in Atlanta. It's not super cheap to live there, but I've never been a party girl or fancy."

"Starbucks connections?" Katie suggested.

"I'm not copying their menu, but if I get on their radar trying to use their discount or anything, I could get my old manager in trouble...or end up with them watching me to be sure I'm not ripping them off." I wasn't looking for trouble.

Katie shook her head. "You'd never do that. Honestly, who isn't doing fancy coffee these days? Fast-food places have crazy coffees. But you're too Goody Two-Shoes. Fine, but at least take some stirrers and napkins. I get a bulk discount, but most people here order beer, so the stirrers only get used with fancy girly drinks."

A cute male bartender leaned over. "Miss, what can I get you?"

"Sorry, Adam, this is my best friend in the whole world—Belle Baxter. Her grandmother owns Baxter Preserves. She drinks for free," Katie said.

"No," I countered.

"She's the boss. What can I get for you, Miss Belle?" Adam asked.

"Water with lime, please." I grinned.

"Please don't be a brat," Katie said. "Cherry Coke. Rum when she's being adventurous."

I was predictable. "No rum tonight, thanks."

Adam fixed my drink and I tucked a five-dollar bill in the tip jar.

"Brat," Katie said.

Adam moved on to tend to other patrons.

"He's cute," I said.

"So is his girlfriend. High school sweethearts." Katie mocked sticking a finger down her throat to mark the grossly perfect couple. "Oh, the band is setting up. Check them out!"

Katie wiped her hands, grabbed her tablet from the back shelf and turned off the music playing throughout the bar. The jukebox in the corner was apparently just for show.

Katie ran over to the alcove of a stage on the far side of the dance floor.

"Good evening and welcome to the Honey Buckle! Live music three nights a week. The best country and blues digital jukebox every night. Line dancing for newbies is on Mondays, so if you want to learn, we can teach you. Tonight, it's a newer band for us, but you keep wanting them around. Snakebite!" Katie announced.

I applauded and there were hoots and hollers, even a few whistles. It was an all-guy band and the lead singer was worth looking at, with his longer hair and muscled arms. He played guitar. The band also had a bass player, along with a guy on keyboard and one on the drums. They were all good-looking men, but it was the guy on the twelve-string who caught my eye.

He stood a bit apart from the rest of the band. He didn't look at the crowd but at his guitar. Tall, dark and handsome was such a cliché, but he was over six feet tall with brown eyes and short dark-brown hair. He was nicely muscled and his face was chiseled and serious. Jeans, cowboy boots and gray T-shirt — I couldn't fault him in the wardrobe department either. Simple, but he didn't look like he'd just rolled out of bed. He'd look great straight out of bed too, but he wasn't too rumpled with rips in his jeans or shirt. Picky girls like me wanted a certain amount of 'a good guy' with a dash of 'can be a bad boy when needed'.

They were well into their first song when Katie came by to sit next to me.

"Like?" she asked.

"They're good. They can play," I teased.

That was a proper compliment. Everyone in or anywhere around Nashville thought they were the next big thing in country music. Everyone played or sang or something.

"The band came down from Kentucky, but they're good. They're nice to open it up to bring in a guest," she said.

"Who is the guest?" I asked.

"Gus, on the twelve-string. He's new in town. A new deputy, but he hasn't officially started yet. Handsome and single. All the girls are drooling," Katie said.

"Can't blame them," I said.

"You should go for it." Katie nudged me with her elbow.

I snickered. "Please, you should go after him. You've got a great business and you're the prettiest girl in town."

Katie glared at me. "We both took a lot of crap as kids, but no one ever called us ugly."

"Exactly, and now you're successful and love music." I sipped my drink.

"You can actually play music," she teased.

I shook my head. "I've got my hands full now. Men, I don't need that to juggle too."

"Soon enough you'll have a handle on things and you'll wish you'd have pounced when he was new in town. He won't be single for long," she pointed out.

"You're saying that I should grab him and reel him in before he knows about my family and reputation?" I asked softly.

"Ugh, I'd never. Your mom screwed up, not you. Your dad is a dead-beat sperm donor but you're a good person," she said.

"We both know that's not how small towns work. I tried leaving, but I won't be my mom. I won't abandon Gran. Speaking of, I should go home. She won't really sleep until I'm home," I said.

Katie rolled her eyes. "We're not in high school anymore. You're grown and can go to a bar with your friends."

"I know. But I have a couple errands to do and an early morning. No fuss, testing out some things for now. We'll do your grand reopening once I've got some things sorted." I hugged her and downed the rest of my Coke.

* * * *

The next morning, I was at the shop early with all my supplies. I blended up a batch of smoothies and put them in little sample cups. Writing up a sign for the smoothie options and pricing, I heard the door.

"Belle, what is the rush?" Gran asked.

The smell of fresh baking was wonderful. "We're going to change things up a bit. It'll take two shakes of a lamb's tail."

"Smoothies?" she asked.

"You said people were asking. I've got some teas too, but we'll start with these. And one other thing." I went over to the coffee and started the pots, but I took down the free coffee sign.

"Annabelle," Gran said.

I put up a new sign that said *Coffee With Free Refills, One Dollar With Purchase Or Three Dollars*, then grabbed the cups and moved them behind the counter.

"It's not unreasonable," I replied.

She put out her signature biscuits and some cinnamon raisin bread.

"People won't be happy," she said.

"Gran, you have a loan to repay and the house will need a new roof in a few years. If you want to bake for charity or for church gatherings for free, that's fine. This is a business. If anyone flies off the handle, you send them to me."

"The boys aren't wrong about social security. Pension and investment stuff is different, but earning money is capped," she said uneasily.

I turned and grabbed both of her wrinkled little hands. "You said you wanted me in on this business too, right?"

"Of course. It's our business. Baxter is on the sign," she said.

"Then we can change how the business is owned if you get anywhere near that earnings cap. If we co-own it, then you only claim half the profits," I explained. "Problem solved."

"But if you make it very successful…" She trailed off.

"When we're in high cotton, you retire, keep hanging out with your boys here as much as you want and help out if you like, but I take it over legally and you'll still get your social security. Then we'll definitely have enough to cover the roof, the loan, and ongoing expenses." I hoped it'd be that simple.

"You don't have to do this. My loan and my house, they're my expenses," she said.

I went to the door and flipped the sign. "That's not how family works. You're not asking me to pay rent. Our house, our business and our expenses. Now crack open those preserves."

The door opened and Mr. Jones walked in with his two pre-teen daughters.

"Dad, come on," Addie whined.

"I need biscuits. The wife is out of town," Mr. Jones said to Gran.

"Cinnamon raisin bread today, too, girls," Gran announced.

The girl had their eyes on their phones with earbuds in.

"Charging for coffee now?" Mr. Jones dropped a bill on the counter. "Smart. Keep the change."

I handed him a cup and travel top. "Mr. Jones, haven't seen you in a coon's age. We can do a hazelnut or caramel flavor shot too," I offered.

"I'm good with black. That's a good call, Belle. Girls, look up. Smoothies." He tapped his daughters on the shoulder.

"No way," Allie said.

The two girls, a year apart in age, acted like twins and were clearly among the cool girls.

They tried the samples. "Nice. We need four."

"Four coming up." I fired up the blender.

Gran's jaw dropped once the customers were gone.

"That's a lot of money for some blended berries and milk. And they took four," she said.

I smiled. "The more customized and personalized we can get, the more we can charge. They probably wanted to get some for friends — being in on a new thing is very teenager."

The boys strolled in and Gran made a fuss about the changes and how they'd better pay up and spread the word. The four guys tried the smoothies and Milan and Joe were brave enough try the flavored coffee shots.

"Fancy," Freddie said.

"It's a start," I countered.

My huge smile was hurting my cheeks, but the bell over the door jingled and my smile was suddenly as fake as a pageant contestant.

Lurlene had walked in. The evil popular girl who'd latched on to tormenting me as a kid and never let up. She still looked perfect.

"Belle Baxter. I heard you were back." She leaned over the counter to air-kiss my cheeks.

I hated the fake girls!

"I am. So kind of you to track me down to mend fences. Coffee? Smoothie?" I offered.

"Interesting. I knew you'd be back to serve us all one day." She sampled a smoothie.

"I'm shocked you're still here. I thought you'd be long gone and married to some rich, important guy by now," I said.

It was pretty much her plan and HS year book quote. She was going to marry well and move to Nashville at the least, take care of her parents and have gorgeous kids.

"I'm picky. You can't rush true love to the right man," she said.

"That's true," Gran agreed.

"Like your mom and her tragic story. Did you ever find her, by the way?" Lurlene took a second sample.

I counted to ten. "I went to college. I wasn't looking for anyone. Gran is all the family I need."

"And you kept that dirty blonde hair. Brave." She reached for another sample.

"Vanity is a sixth sense. Can I get you something?" I offered.

My hair was on the dirty blonde side and Lurlene loved to say it. Her blonde was perfect and straight out of a bottle. She viewed me as some weird competition, according to Katie. We both had long wavy hair, blue eyes, pale skin, and petite figures. Lurlene was a few inches taller.

"I suppose I'll take a smoothie. Skim milk unless you have almond milk," she said.

"Not yet. We're still expanding the menu, but thanks for the suggestion." I blended her up a berry smoothie and rang her up.

"Biscuits, dear?" Gran offered.

"Oh no, no carbs. Thank you," Lurlene said.

"Bye, dear," Gran said.

I'd be annoyed, but Lurlene had never been rude to my grandmother that I'd ever seen. Then again, I'd never done anything to Lurlene that I was aware of and she'd decided that I was the enemy.

"What's she doing now, Gran?" I asked after Lurlene was out of the door.

"Oh, she works at her dad's store. It's mostly tractor supply and feed. I buy Duke's puppy food there. They support local business too. I can't complain, but she's always been jealous of you." Gran shrugged it off.

Jealous wasn't the word I'd use. Her family was intact and flawless, from what I knew. But I didn't know everything about my own family, so who was I to make assumptions?

Milan smirked. "Lurlene wants to marry the pastor. She talked about college when you first went, but there was always a young man she didn't want to lose out on. Or her dad needed her help."

"Helping her dad is good." If I couldn't say anything nice, I'd keep quiet, but that was polite enough.

"She wants to be taken care of," Joe agreed. "Poor girl grew up with an old-school father. His way or it's wrong. Mother keeps a perfect house but doesn't work except when the family business needs her. She never said a peep. Lurlene and her sister didn't know how to make a decision on their own. Your gran was a free thinker compared to some."

"Everyone has their faults and challenges. Belle, don't you forget about the pastor and choir. You need to play piano," Gran reminded me.

"This afternoon. I'll put a reminder in my phone." I pulled out my cell and programmed a reminder.

While things were quiet, I shopped online for a small fridge and a slightly used coffee machine.

Before I could pick a model, the door opened and a group came in. Word was getting around. People in small towns where nothing changed loved new options. I mentally made a note to get a couple of big blenders, because Katie's little one might be dead by lunch.

* * * *

I walked into the church and wandered around a bit. I checked the choir room and the pastor's office. Finally, I found the pastor in the main church, where the piano was.

"Hope I'm not late," I said.

"No, not at all, Ms. Baxter. Please get comfortable with your instrument." Pastor Nelson vacated the chair. "There's some music set out for you."

I took the bench and flipped through the sheet music. Nothing too tricky. Standard really.

"Thank you, Pastor, but call me Belle. I am a bit rusty. I didn't have my keyboard in Atlanta. I should've taken it, but between working and classes, there wasn't much time to practice anyway," I admitted.

"It's okay, and you can call me Luke. We've been muddling through without anyone since Mrs. Armstrong retired to Arizona." He sat in the first pew. "Whenever you're ready."

Luke? That was way too familiar for a pastor I'd just met. Respecting the elderly was critical, but religious men got a lot of it too. It was just habit. I'd figure out the name thing later. He was good-looking and focused on his work without being stuffy or condescending.

I wiggled my fingers and tuned out the rest of the world. I focused on the music and forgot anyone was listening. Piano was normal for me. I'd had lessons since I was four until fourteen because Gran had seen that I loved music. She'd steered me hard away from guitars or drums and toward the piano. I often wondered if my mom ran off with a musician or my father had been one. Maybe the rumor of my mom being musical was true?

It didn't really matter. On the piano, I could play any sort of music, and a small keyboard was just as portable as a guitar.

Two songs in, I heard applause. My fingers froze.

"Thanks," I said.

"You don't need to do any more. You are more than talented enough to accompany our choir. Practice starts soon. I hope you can stay." The pastor walked up the steps.

"How often is practice?" I asked.

"Once a week for two hours. But it's afternoons so shouldn't cut into the busy time at your gran's shop. Of course, Sunday mornings at ten is our service, which is the big show, but Beatrice usually closes for service." He held out his hand. "We're blessed to have your talent."

"Thanks again, Pastor. Glad to help. I'll just let Gran know not to expect me back soon." I shook his hand and felt the extra squeeze he gave.

"Luke, please. None of these church ladies will stop with the formality," he said.

Was the pastor flirting with me? I grabbed my phone and felt weird about using it here. "I'll go into the entryway to make the call."

I glanced back and he waved. He was grinning pretty wide.

Pastor Luke was good-looking and my age, but it felt a bit odd. If I somehow upended Lurlene's plans for the pastor, I'd be the most enthusiastic piano player Sweet Grove Community Church had ever seen.

Chapter Four

Avoiding the parade of church-goers and the small talk was another perk of playing for the service. I was decked out in a nice green dress and brown flats. My hair was pulled back and the choir ladies had commented approvingly. We hung out in the back until service started, so no doubt Gran was fielding all sorts of questions about where I was.

She was most definitely telling them where I was with pride. For me, it was about the music and maybe the cute pastor. But a little bit of it had to be about acceptance too. None of the choir ladies had asked about my mother or father. They'd only made polite conversation about my time in Atlanta so far.

"Ready, ladies?" Luke walked out, looking very sharp in a dark gray suit.

Service began and I tried not to think about anything but the music and my cues.

When playing piano, I could easily get lost in the music. Any sort of music, really. I liked a variety, but even tried and true church music was fine when I needed a break from reality. Playing at church had only one problem — it meant most of the town was there and watching. Gossip that I was back had surely spread on day one, but now I was on display.

My focus remained on sitting up straight and not playing so loudly that I overpowered the choir. The sermon about the prodigal son seemed a bit prickly and on point.

Finally, the service was nearly over. I wouldn't be a novelty anymore and we could just be normal.

"A few closing remarks and announcements. I'd like to thank Belle Baxter for taking up the piano duties for our service and choir. She's expanding the menu over at Bea Baxter's shop, so check out the smoothies and coffee offerings. It's lovely to have family businesses in town and we should support them. Wholesome homemade baked goods and an array of beverages that are kid-friendly — we need more of that. One last reminder to be the olive branch for your own prodigal sons and daughters and to support those who return. Go with God." Pastor nodded.

I played some music as people filed out, but my fingers wanted to hit the keys harder than I should. Was I prodigal? The sales plug seemed like charity. I tried to remember my marketing, that there was no such thing as bad publicity. I glanced at the crowd and felt their stares.

One man caught my eye, and he wasn't staring at me with pity or annoyance.

That guitar player who was the new deputy, according to Katie. Handsome and sitting alone — in church. If he was single, he wouldn't be for long.

I also spotted Lurlene and her family. She sat with her parents and sister, who'd already gotten married.

That must've stung. Surely Gran had mentioned the wedding, but I blocked out most of that information about them to keep my sanity.

I pressed my lips together to avoid smiling. Lurlene was staring at the pastor like he was next on her list. *Good luck!*

After church, there was a social hour of sorts with coffee and pastries. Gran, of course, had brought some preserves and rolls.

After chatting with the choir ladies, who seemed pleased, I tried to sneak out.

"Belle, you have to stay and mingle," the pastor said.

"Thanks, but that boost you gave the shop will probably create a stampede," I said.

"I wanted to help get the word out." He blushed.

Oh, was he crushing on me while Lurlene circled him like a vulture? That was the last thing I needed — but it was awfully nice.

"I appreciate the mention — we'll have to have you over for dinner. But you don't need to say anything again. It's a small town and people know everything about everything so quickly. I don't want people thinking that I'm looking for charity. You understand."

"See you at practice and next week," he replied.

"Sure. Thank you." I found Gran and hustled her away to the shop.

* * * *

The shop wasn't packed, but it was certainly busier. I liked the Danish that Gran had made for the day and my smoothies were a hit. Kids dragged their parents in, using the pastor as an excuse. If it was good enough for a man of the cloth...right?

Gran beamed when the pastor came in and ordered a large mint julep smoothie.

It slowed down around noon. Sunday lunch or dinner with the family, depending on schedules, was a thing. But Gran had packed us a picnic basket of fried chicken and homemade mashed potatoes. Comfort food, if a bit traditional.

"This is so good, Gran," I said.

She grinned. "I don't know why we needed to leave the church so fast. I like socializing."

"Sorry, but after the pastor's remarks, I knew we'd have some kids at least wanting to try something new." I stood up a little straighter. "Next week you can hang back and talk up the specials for that day."

"I can do that. I'm not sure how much business you'll get this afternoon. Family time," she warned.

I finished my lunch then put the silverware back in the basket. After tossing out the trash, I washed my hands. "I know, but your hours are until four, so we might as well see. Some parents might make the kids wait until after lunch and the smoothie is like a dessert."

Gran straightened up the counter. "Smart. The boys will be in soon. They always visit after lunch at the diner. They're so predictable."

"Why don't you go to lunch with them?" I asked.

"I used to, but you're here now." She grabbed my hand.

"Gran, you don't have to change your life for me. I want you to enjoy your friends and everything. I just want to be here if you need me." I wiped down the counter.

"I'm not helpless. I'm not arguing, because I like having you back, but I'm fine. You didn't need to move.

Sometimes I get tired when I have too much to do and I forget one thing. One time I forgot to fold the laundry in the dryer for a whole week. I wondered why I was running so low on towels." She chuckled.

"Then don't let me stop you from going out to lunch with the boys next week. I don't think we'll have a lunch rush and I can grab something from the diner or pack my own lunch." I wanted her to enjoy her golden years, but the reality was that things wouldn't get better. She'd forget more and grow more tired — I'd rather be here than get a terrifying call.

The door opened and Gran's four men piled in. Her smile said it all. They'd brought her pudding from the diner.

I fussed over cleaning the already clean blenders so Gran and her harem could all chat without including me. *Since when am I the fifth wheel, or sixth in this case?* At least she hadn't been lonely without me.

The door opened again and a bunch of people poured in.

"We talked you up to the diner crowd," Joe said.

"Thanks," I replied.

Half an hour of nonstop flavored coffees and smoothies and I was beat.

Just as I checked the time, hoping to flip the sign on the door, Sheriff Monroe and his wife strolled in.

"Good afternoon. What can I get for you?" I asked.

"Been behaving yourself?" The sheriff answered my question with a question.

I was on my best behavior. "Absolutely. Working and playing piano in church. We missed you there."

His wife shot him a look. "I had a migraine but managed to kick it."

"That's good. We have a triple berry or a mint julep smoothie, or flavored coffees on top of Gran's usual delights." I gestured to the food, but it was getting late in the day for that. The pastries were probably a tad stale by now.

"I'll try the berry," Mrs. Monroe said. "This is something new, but do you think the trends will last?'

I put my hands on my hips and gave a moment's thought. "Adapting to what people want is part of the business. Some people have asked for blended coffee drinks."

"I'll try a mint julep," the sheriff ordered.

I blended up the drinks and handed them over. The sheriff reached for his wallet.

"No, no charge for police," Gran insisted.

She was sharp when she wanted to be. It was common practice.

"No need. That's kind, but we like to help." The sheriff tried to pay.

I shook my head with a polite smile. "On the house. You heard the boss."

"Thanks." They sipped their drinks, seemed pleased and headed out.

Behind them was the twelve-string guitar player guy.

"Hello again," he said.

"Hi, I don't think we've been introduced," I replied.

He reached out a hand. "Gus Haywood. I saw you at the bar."

"Right, you were playing. I'm Belle Baxter. Gran and her entourage are over there." I pointed.

Gran waved. "Nice to have some new men around."

"Katie said you're a new deputy, I believe. Unless I'm mixing up the band members." I didn't want to seem fixated on the new guy. All the band members were new to me anyway.

"No, that's me. I'm not really a part of that band. I just like to sit in. It's good practice. Like you in church," he said.

"Yes, practice never hurts. What can I get you?" I offered.

"I'll try the mint julep. Interesting little town," he said.

I blended his drink and gave it to him with a bit of a chuckle. "How is Sweet Grove interesting?"

"Not many chain restaurants."

"True, we support local businesses more. There are a few fast-food places on the outskirts of town by the expressway ramps. Main Street doesn't allow it," I explained.

"It's nice, but I do miss a good coffee drive-thru. They're everywhere in Atlanta and Nashville."

I looked around. "You're from Atlanta? I went to college there and worked for a bit. How funny."

"Small world. I started out there. Moved to Tennessee and worked in Nashville." He shrugged.

"Big cities," I countered.

"What brought you here?" Milan asked.

Gus chuckled. "I got tired of the big city. I grew up in the suburbs of Atlanta, but big-city police politics isn't what I'm interested in. I wanted to help people. Get to know the people."

"You might not need as much coffee. Things are a bit slower around here," Gran said.

"Caffeine is my only addiction. I can't give it up," he said.

"Not sure I can make this a drive-thru, but I'm considering getting a fancy coffee machine. I worked at a Starbucks in college, so I know how to make anything, though I'd customize it my own way, of course. Still, I need the right machine. Good to know there is some demand. People might judge you for your fancy coffee," I warned him.

He chuckled. "I'm not worried about that. Caffeine is necessary and trying a variety keeps things interesting."

"If you're easily bored, you might not like Sweet Grove," Milan called out.

I studied Gus when he went over and introduced himself to Gran's gentlemen friends. He had a casual but positive energy. He chatted easily with the seniors and came over, reaching for his wallet.

"I didn't forget," he said.

"Nope, on the house. Gran doesn't charge law enforcement," I said.

"Thanks, but I haven't officially started yet," Gus replied.

"Then it's a welcome-to-town drink," Gran added.

"Hopefully I'll get that coffee machine and you'll be a regular," I suggested.

He put a five-dollar bill on the counter. "You need a tip jar."

"No, that's silly for a bakery shop," Gran said.

"Thank you, Mr. Haywood. He's right, Gran, donut shops in Atlanta have them. All the coffee places do," I shared.

"Call me Gus." He lifted his drink as he headed for the door.

"Deputy," Joe suggested.

Gus sighed. "Soon enough."

"Deputy," I agreed. When the seniors used titles for respect, I wasn't going to push past that to more familiar terms. But Gus sounded better.

The door jingled and closed.

"He's handsome and well-mannered," Gran said.

"Unlike most of the deputies," Freddie chuckled.

"The sheriff will love him. Big-city experience and not in it for power." I cleaned up the blenders.

"You got that right," Milan scoffed. "Unless people like him better than the sheriff."

"Are you guys taking Gran out for dinner?" I teased.

"Oh no, she never does big dinner stuff because she has to work so early. We'll take her to lunch tomorrow," Joe replied.

"Okay, good. I'll make pasta." I needed a routine and was going to make plans. I grabbed one of Gran's large empty preserve jars and set it on the counter. Dropping the five-dollar bill in the jar, I couldn't argue with the suggestion. I didn't label the jar for tips, but having it out was a signal. This was my business now too and we had to play to some of the trends while keeping the small-town feel.

* * * *

Monday morning, I still had mint julep on the menu and the berries were still good. I prepped the coffee and hummed, hoping Deputy Gus might stop in again.

Gran arranged her cinnamon rolls along with her traditional biscuits.

"Some people like biscuits and gravy," I mentioned.

"It's the south, dear. Lots of people do." Gran sipped her own coffee.

"But you're one of the best cooks in Tennessee. You could put out your gravy one morning just for a change," I said.

She chuckled. "This is a preserves shop, not a breakfast stand."

"I know, but I'm adding smoothies and coffee. Making one morning all about your famous biscuits and gravy might bring people in," I said.

"Your drinks are nice things to accompany the breakfast goodies. Which accent my preserves."

Only my Gran could believe she'd sustain a shop on her preserves alone. I'd told her many times to do that out of her house and at fests over the summer. She liked her storefront.

It was five minutes before opening time and someone knocked on the door.

I peeked through the beige blinds and it was Milan.

I opened the door and all four guys piled in.

"Oh dear, you're not going to believe it," Freddie said.

"What?" I brushed off my apron decorated with large pictures of fruit and tossed it behind the counter.

"Bea, it's not a good day," Joe warned.

"What is it? We're not mind readers," she replied.

"Sheriff Monroe is dead," Milan announced.

"What?" Gran and I gasped together.

"Well, shut my mouth," I muttered.

"He started vomiting and complaining of stomach pain after dinner last night. His wife had him rushed to the hospital in Nashville. He died on the way," Freddie sighed.

Gran sat down with the guys. "Nashville. What's wrong with our little hospital here?"

"You know how she is. The city is better," Milan replied.

"Well, there are more medical resources there. But if you don't make it there in time, it's no good." I tried not to worry about what Gran might need one day.

"They're doing an autopsy. He had his physical a month ago and he was fine," Joe said.

I frowned. "How do you know that?"

"Law enforcement requires annual physicals for insurance and everything. I'm a former deputy," Freddie explained.

"Weird that he got sick so fast," I said.

"He wasn't in the best shape. A heart attack can come out of nowhere." Gran refilled her coffee.

"They're saying he was vomiting, and a bunch of other stuff suddenly. Mrs. Monroe swears it was poison." Milan shook his head.

"I'm sure the deputies will be investigating the restaurant where they had dinner." I flipped the sign on the door and opened it since the weather was nice.

There was no one out there.

"I'm not sure you'll get much business today." Freddie frowned.

"What do you mean?" I asked.

Just then Deputy Henshaw walked in.

"Good morning. Mrs. Baxter." He tipped his hat. "Belle, sorry."

"Morning, Deputy. You're sorry about what exactly?" Mike Henshaw and I had been in high school together. He'd been popular and I hadn't, but he'd never been really mean like some. Still, he was being extra nice now.

"I'm afraid we need to confiscate your blenders and ingredients for the mint julep smoothies. For further testing. I'm sure it's all fine," he said.

"What? Plenty of people had smoothies. Was he allergic to anything? There's no nuts or anything in there, but people can be allergic to anything," I rambled.

"No allergies, according to his doc, and there was no visible allergic reaction." Mike shook his head.

"You can't think…" I was a suspect? "It's crazy. I had no ax to grind with him."

"I know, but we have to be thorough. The medical examiner is running a tox screen and they're going to check everything, but we can't let anyone destroy evidence — just in case," Mike said.

"Take what you want, but that other deputy had the same thing right after the sheriff," Gran scolded.

"Which deputy?" Mike asked.

"Gus. He said he hasn't officially started yet." I gestured to behind the counter. "Help yourself. Can we still serve coffee and preserves?"

"Sheriff have any yesterday?" Mike asked.

"No," Gran replied.

"Then you're fine. We'll get to the bottom of this as soon as we can, I promise. We had to shut down the restaurant to be sure. That's a lot of testing and sampling. This is crazy. I can't believe he's gone." Mike adjusted his hat.

"I'm so sorry he's gone, but no one else reported any illness from anything they had here. I didn't do anything differently. I have nothing against the sheriff." I shrugged.

"We know he pulled you over your first night back," Mike replied.

"He's pulled nearly everyone in town over at one point or another. Plus, he let me off with a warning. It wasn't a big deal," I said.

"He said you were really annoyed with him." Mike went out and returned with a box.

Gran huffed. "The sheriff ate terribly and smoked when his wife wasn't looking."

"Then the autopsy will show it, Gran. We have nothing to hide," I said.

"That's the right attitude. We'll take a more formal statement later, but right now I just need to take possession before evidence is destroyed. I'll be out of your way in a few." Mike went behind the counter.

I sat in the front without customers. Was this a sign?

My phone binged. I expected a message from Katie. Instead it was a notification that my coffee machine had shipped.

Perfect timing!

Chapter Five

It'd been a few days and there was no news. No one else had even gotten a little sick, so food poisoning was ruled out. The entire town was on edge but no one else had died. Clearly it was personal — whoever had killed the sheriff was only after him.

Gran had fallen asleep early and I needed to get out.

I walked into the packed bar and found that it didn't help my mood at all. People were looking at me.

Katie waved me over and found me a spot. "Hey, you look like you need a drink."

"Business has been slow. It's not that way here." I looked around with a teensy bit of envy.

Katie looked around. "People want to forget when bad things happen, especially things that they can't control or explain."

"They think you did it," Lurlene said from a few spots down.

"Please. That dog won't hunt." I shook my head.

Katie bit her lower lip.

"Really? What reason could they possibly think I'd have to want to hurt the sheriff?" I asked.

Lurlene pursed her lips. "He pulled you over. Maybe you just wanted to make him sick? A little payback for police harassment. Maybe you put in too much poison?"

My jaw dropped. "I'd never poison anyone. How could people think that?"

Katie scoffed. "It was probably a heart attack or something. Natural. The guy drank, smoked and had a bad diet."

Deputy Lou Foster sauntered up to the bar and took the stool between me and Lurlene. "Ladies." He touched the brim of his hat.

"What'll you have, Lou?" Katie asked.

"Coke. I'm always on call now," Lou said.

"Any news?" I asked.

Lou sighed. He wasn't the cleverest of the deputies, but he was the most likely to spill things he shouldn't. "Nothing really. Just ruled out some things."

Gus walked up and stood next to me. He felt so tall and solid standing close by. "Ladies, Lou. What's the good word?"

Lou shot Gus an annoyed glance but covered quickly with a sip of his drink. "I was just going to update the ladies. Post-mortem said his heart gave out, but his physical said nothing was wrong so they're still looking. Something else killed him."

"Any poison in that blender of yours, Belle?" Lurlene teased.

"If there were, I'd be dead. I had the same thing as the sheriff, made not five minutes later," Gus defended.

I tried not to blush. Gus was the man every woman was talking about, but he wasn't just good-looking—he was kind and honest. But the dark brown hair and slight stubble made it hard to focus on his character.

"A deputy for an alibi. Whatever did you do to get him so firmly on your side?" Lurlene asked.

"An officer of the law can't be bribed," Lou jumped in.

Gus nodded. "He's right. At least a good one can't. There were plenty of witnesses to the sheriff and me being there."

Lurlene shot me a look. "They're checking everyone, but come on. She worked at Starbucks and had to make drinks fast. All the customers out from socializing while she's behind the counter working the machines. I have full faith that Belle could've slipped a special ingredient into the sheriff's smoothie after it was blended. Powder or something. Or even blend it in then swap out the pitcher for another one before she made any else's drink. I could never work that fast."

"Working fast doesn't make someone a murderer," Lou replied.

I got the sense that Lou wasn't in a rush to solve anything. He liked the attention, the power and the intrigue.

"Fast doesn't mean easy either," Katie snarked at Lurlene.

"You fast girls do stick together." Lurlene put money on the bar. "Gus, would you walk me to my car?"

"Allow me." Lou stood up.

"But...thanks." Lurlene fumbled for a polite way back to the man she wanted to get alone.

"It's part of my job. I'm working here a bit, security on a trial basis." Lou looked at Katie.

"It's true. One of my half-brothers started community college and his schedule sucks. Lou is helping," she replied.

Lurlene smiled. "Well, this is a friendly favor, not a job."

Gus stood up straight, like he'd oblige. "I'm not sure we know each other well enough to be friends, but I'm certainly not going to step on Lou's toes. Katie should get what she paid for and I should work on making friends here."

Lurlene was stuck as Lou offered his arm.

Being a polite southern lady sometimes cornered a woman. I'd been there. I almost felt sorry for her, but Lou wasn't drunk or creepy. She started to leave. I gave her a little wave and turned to Gus.

"That woman could start an argument in an empty house," I scoffed.

"The problem is, who else has motive?" Katie said once they were gone.

Gus sighed. "I wish we had a better lead. He didn't do anything out of the ordinary that day except the smoothie."

"But Belle would never hurt a fly," Katie insisted.

Gus grinned at me and I had to look away. This guy was too good to be true. He had flaws—I just had to find them. Gran's advice on marriage was finding someone a person loved enough to put up with their bad habits and quirks, because no one was perfect. Gus' looks and musical interests were pros…but there had to be some cons somewhere.

"I believe it, and plenty of people had access to the sheriff. Poison can be passed in other ways, not just food. But why would anyone want to kill him? He's been elected in a landslide year after year, according to what I've heard," Gus said.

"But you're new. No one is going to talk bad about the sheriff to a new deputy," Katie pointed out.

"Who would have a grudge against Monroe?" Gus asked.

I shared a look with Katie. "I mean, obviously someone else wants that job. Plenty of people, I'm sure. But to kill over it? That's crazy."

"Some people become obsessed over things. Something not that big to others feels intensely personal to someone else," Gus replied. "Obviously they'll be looking at people he put into jail who are now free."

"That makes way more sense," I agreed.

"We definitely don't know the sheriff that well. I don't know his secrets," Katie said.

"Exactly. I didn't raise my voice to the sheriff when he pulled me over. Why would I do anything to hurt him over a warning?" I sipped whatever Katie had put in front of me.

"That makes no sense. Is your grandmother doing okay?" Gus asked.

"She's worried about the sheriff's widow. Business has been down and she's worried about that but won't say it. She does appreciate your breakfast business," I replied.

"Home-cooked pastry is hard to beat. It's pretty busy still," Gus remarked.

"Sure, for her coffee and pastries. The smoothies are dead. I even bought a new blender since Katie's is still in police custody for some reason." I stirred my drink mindlessly.

Gus put his hand on my arm and I tried not to jump as my skin tingled.

"They don't have the tox screen back. If they find something, they'll be trying to match it up with anything and everything. The diner still has pots and pans in evidence," Gus said.

"Thanks," I replied.

"I'm lucky he didn't come in that day or the night before. He usually drinks bottled beer, but they'd be accusing us of slipping him a mickey." Katie shook her head.

"They?" Gus prompted.

"Gossips in town. Girls from the wrong side of the tracks will always get the blame." Katie went to service more patrons.

"Which side is the right side?" Gus asked.

I chuckled. "Sweet Grove isn't laid out like that exactly. Gran is a staple of the community, but the Baxters have never been well off. Then my mom came along and was sort of wild. That kind of thing — you're only as good as your most embarrassing relation. Now, if you're rich, you get away with more."

"I can't believe that," Gus said.

"Then you're not paying attention to gossip. Which is a good trait, but if you're going to be a deputy, you have to deal in how people do act, not just how they should," I teased.

Gus leaned on the bar. He smelled good in a hard-to-pin-down way, with a hint of pine trees. He was in jeans and boots with a gray dress shirt open at the collar and rolled up at the sleeves.

"I filter information just fine. Rumor and gossip can be remembered without being given credit. Everyone has an agenda. They all have an angle and their own goals and priorities," he replied.

"I don't have an angle," I defended.

"Saving your Gran's business isn't an angle?" he asked.

I shook my head. "No, it's a goal, sure. Small businesses are getting edged out and it's harder to turn a profit. She's getting older. Maybe I should've just convinced her to sell her house and the shop and move to Atlanta with me. At least then we wouldn't be poor as field mice."

Gus was quiet for a moment and I wished I hadn't said that. Did it make me seem guilty? I hoped not, but it did make me seem desperate and afraid. I didn't want him thinking I liked him and was looking to land a man for stability.

"I'm glad you didn't. I might have missed out." He sipped his drink.

"Missed out?" Katie came back at just the wrong time.

"On Gran's great pastries…if they had closed the shop during the investigation. That would be such a bummer. Luckily the sheriff only had a smoothie. Small towns need their core eateries," I said.

Katie nodded. "She should make it a donut shop or something."

"I like the fancy coffee and I'm man enough to admit it," Gus said.

That manly to own it, here? He was great. *Too good to be true.*

Another bartender rang a bell over the bar. "Last call."

"It can't be that late." Gus checked his phone.

He had a few texts from a pretty, redheaded young woman, but I glanced away. He was probably taken and his girlfriend was just settling her job before she moved to Sweet Grove.

"Sorry we talked your ear off." I hopped off the stool. "I'll help clean up, Katie."

"Thanks, but you don't have to." Katie sighed as she watched half the bar settle their tabs and head for the door. The other half ordered one last round. "It has been crazy busy tonight."

"See? You need the help." I finished my drink then went around behind the bar and bussed the glass.

"One more?" Katie asked Gus.

"No, I'm fine. Good night." He dropped payment on the bar.

Katie shook her head. "No charge."

"That's not a smart way to do business." Gus headed for the door.

An hour later, we were largely cleaned up as far as tables and bar top went. The other bartenders were stocking for the next day. I was sweeping the floors while Katie polished the brass on the bar and the door handle.

"Gus really seems to like you," Katie teased.

I rolled my eyes. "I'm not getting my hopes up. It was enough that Lurlene didn't get her claws into him yet."

Katie giggled and sighed. "Just be careful. I think those deputies would be thrilled to pin it all on you."

"Why? I mean, I get they want to solve it, but they want the real killer. I hope it was all just a big accident," I said.

"An accident? How?" she asked.

"If nothing from the diner, my stuff or the sheriff's home tests positive for poison, maybe he got something some other way? Maybe he accidentally took too much of a medication. Someone could've slipped him a medication or spiked a drink," I suggested.

"Like GHB. Some women won't accept drinks from men even if I take it over. They don't trust it hasn't been tampered with. They want bottled water that's sealed. They open their own beer bottles. Usually they're visitors, but it freaked me out the first time," Katie said.

"That's all the time in the city. Locals are trusting of each other. But it's possible someone could've done that to the sheriff's coffee or anything, really. I guess we have to wait for the tox screen," I said.

Katie held up her hand. "If I were you, I'd get back to normal. Make your smoothies and coffee drinks."

"It won't be tacky?" I asked.

"Name one after the sheriff. Like in tribute. You did nothing wrong and you know it. You'll be at the funeral, but you know you're innocent and the business must go on." Katie put her hands on her hips like a superhero.

"Thanks. I needed that. I think I will." I grabbed the dustpan and brushed the dirt into it. "People are still going to try to blame me."

"You just got back into town. No mysterious deaths before that. I know it's a coincidence, but you have that going against you over every other person in Sweet Grove," she pointed out.

"Darn right," I agreed as I dumped the dirt into the trash can.

"Thanks for the help. Go home and get some sleep. You have an early morning," she said.

"Always. I've learned to live on less sleep." I grabbed my purse and headed out to my truck.

There was a note under the windshield wiper. I grabbed it and unfolded the piece of paper.

Cowardly Killer

I didn't recognize the handwriting. Probably a joke from Lurlene to try to get rid of me.

Coming home was always going to be hard, but this was taking the cake! I crumpled up the paper and hopped in my truck. Tossing the paper and my purse into the passenger seat, I had the keys in my hand. I took a moment to breathe then shoved the key into the ignition and turned.

I drove toward home with a slight detour past the shop. There was a big box on the porch. Why would someone deliver something to the front of a business?

I parked the truck around back and went inside. Once I'd opened the front door and used my body to hold it open, I slid the heavy box inside. The shades were all down and I immediately locked the front door behind me before I proceeded to push, kick, nudge and shove the large box behind the counter. I didn't need Gran tripping on it or trying to move it if she decided to beat me in to work in the morning.

I heard the door rattle.

Ducking down, I slid the box where it was totally out of the way and peeked over the counter.

I saw a figure trying the door. I kept silent and they went away. Only then did I approach the door and make sure all three locks were engaged. I made my way out back and checked the alley before I walked out.

It looked deserted. I locked the door behind me and dashed for my truck. Driving home, I obeyed every speed limit and traffic sign like I'd just gotten my license. No one appeared to be following me.

By the time I parked at Gran's, I felt less paranoid. Someone had been trying to get into the shop. That wasn't my imagination. But who and why?

Maybe there really was a killer loose in Sweet Grove?

Chapter Six

Sleeping hadn't gone all that well, so I was up and at the shop before Gran. Normal coffee was brewed and I'd changed my sign.

Sheriff Monroe Mint Julep Smoothie Special

I cut the price in half and propped up the sign. After prepping my area for the special, I turned to the big box with its fancy coffee maker. The tape on it was industrial strength. I dug through the office drawers for a pair of scissors and scrounged up a box cutter instead.

I walked back to the main area and found Gran and her four admirers sitting and chatting already.

"Wow, it's really quiet back there," I said.

"Morning, dear. Yes, they had some soundproofing put in. It was that way when I rented the space. Helps when you need to make a phone call or do paperwork."

"I bought this new coffee and espresso maker. I'm going to set it up. Don't mean to be rude, but don't mind me." I waved at the men.

Gran came over with a scone on a plate. "Eat some breakfast first. What are you up to?"

"Scones? Are we British now?" I teased.

"I had extra blueberries from the muffins. Things are a tad slow," she said.

"My fault. But I'm not giving up. Smoothies are back on the menu, in memorial, and fancy coffee drinks." I sliced open the box, adjusted down the blade and put the box cutter in my back pocket for safe keeping. "We might be a little slower while they investigate, but things will bounce back."

"None of this is your fault." She patted my cheek.

"Thanks, I just know you need your business to increase and so far, I've not helped a bit." I looked down. "Gran, you're wearing two different shoes."

She looked down. "Oh, navy and black. I need to turn the lights on in the closet. The bulb burned out."

"I'll change it when we get home," I said.

"See? Having you here helps. People like new — it just takes them a bit to adjust. We must remember the poor sheriff and his family. Business can be recovered, but death is forever."

"I'm sorry, I know. I can't fix that, so I'm doing what I can," I replied.

"I know, but you don't need to meddle or change things up right now. Don't need to be riling people up," she said.

"I'm not." I attempted to lift the coffee machine from the box. "Darn."

"We can help." Milan offered.

"Thanks, but I don't want anyone to pull a muscle. It's very heavy," I said.

"We've got this." Milan held up his hands.

The four men studied the project. I sighed and broke off a piece of the scone.

"Belle, I know you're a good girl, but people are talking. You need to lie low," Gran said.

"I didn't do anything. I'm tired of being guilty for nothing that I did." I went to the front door and flipped the sign to open.

Gran supervised the project and I prayed no one here had a heart attack. I'd definitely get the blame.

"They got it out of the box," Gran announced.

I walked over and put down a mat on the counter so the machine wouldn't scratch the wood.

"Much obliged. Let me help." I took a corner.

"You're a tiny thing. It'll crush you," Gran argued.

But I was much younger and not a weakling. I'd seen these things installed and it took a couple of strong men to lift it easily. I had to help.

We tried twice but didn't clear the counter.

We were trying again when the bell over the door jingled.

"Crap!" someone said and the machine slipped to the floor.

"Let's take a break. We'll get some coffee and food in us," I said.

Gran was waiting on the customer. I finally looked over, hoping to find Gus or even the pastor. Any strong young man. But it was Lurlene.

"That is so sweet. You know, Belle, your true calling is in hospitality." Lurlene smiled wide. "But maybe not this."

"Do go on." I refused to take the bait.

"Honestly, no. Think about it. A retirement home might be just the thing for you to run. The smoothies would help for those who have trouble eating. You have the patience for it. You already have five seniors here. You'll never be alone or friendless. There will always be more people getting old. That way you don't have to worry about finding a husband or all of that. Or making a business that is on trend," she mocked but sounded so sincere.

I almost said something rude, but the door opened. Gus and Lou walked in, both in uniform.

Gran pushed scones and coffee on them.

"Official already?" I asked Gus.

"Yes, ma'am. We need to talk, Belle," he replied.

Gran shook her head. "You're not taking her anywhere."

"No, ma'am. We just want to get more information. We can talk in the back," Lou said.

"Shame you're a suspect. Good luck," Lurlene called as she left.

I led them to the back.

Gus paused behind the counter. "Let us help."

He nodded to Lou and they lifted the machine onto the counter.

"Thanks," I said.

In the back office, I sat at the desk.

"Tell us what happened the night you were pulled over," Lou said.

I sighed. "I'm sure there was a report. I guess I was speeding a bit. I was tired and no one was on the road so I wasn't watching my speedometer like a hawk. He pulled me over, I had insurance and registration up to date. He let me off with a warning. That's all."

"Did you see anyone in his police car? Was there anyone around?" Gus asked.

"I didn't see anyone," I answered.

"Did he seem upset or distracted?" Lou asked.

I shook my head. "Nope. He seemed like any other day. I just got back to town, so I don't know if he'd had any problems with anyone lately."

"We've spoken to the widow. She said he complained a lot about your traffic stop," Gus replied.

"That's how slow of a day he had. I usually fall asleep on night patrol." Lou chuckled.

"I'm sure Mrs. Monroe is just beside herself with grief and wants to blame anyone and everyone." I knew Gran had taken pastries to the woman, but beyond that, we couldn't do much to help.

The deputies shared a look. Lou closed his notepad.

That look was weird. Like maybe the widow hadn't been so lost in grief.

"Don't leave the state, Belle. Okay?" Lou asked.

I smirked. "I'm not going anywhere."

The deputies took their scones and coffee to go. Gran and her friends were playing with my new machine.

"Please be careful—I just bought it." I walked up.

"Can we try one?" Gran asked.

"First tell me if Mrs. Monroe was really upset about her husband's death," I said.

Gran frowned. "Of course she was. She didn't show it. It's not ladylike to be sobbing and helpless all the time. Especially with visitors. I'm sure she's had private grieving."

"You're sure, or you're being polite and their marriage wasn't what it used to be?" I asked.

"Belle, that's not our business," Gran said.

"It's not gossip if we're trying to find out who the real killer is." I looked at the time. "I'll take the widow some scones."

"That's nice, dear," Gran said.

"We'll get this set up for you. Men are good with machinery," Milan called.

"Thanks!" I replied. Under my breath, I whispered, "Please don't break it."

* * * *

The sheriff's home was an immaculately maintained white colonial with carved columns on the front porch that gave it an old-school southern feel. The flower boxes were perfectly filled out and the Cadillac in the driveway shone like new.

There was another car parked out front, but it wasn't a police car.

I parked on the street and checked my makeup in the rearview mirror. Scones in hand, I headed up to the front door. Only the screen was shut, so I could see the pastor and Mrs. Monroe sitting in the living room.

"Hello, Belle. How nice of you to visit." Pastor Luke stood up.

"Yes, come in." Mrs. Monroe sounded less enthused than the pastor. "We were discussing funeral plans."

"Sorry to interrupt. I wanted to drop by with some scones." I handed over a container.

"I think we have everything we need. I'll be in touch. If you need anything, Mrs. Monroe, let me know." The pastor headed for the door.

"You don't need to leave," I insisted.

"It's fine. Sit." Mrs. Monroe gestured to her overstuffed La-Z-Boy couch. Not at all what I'd imagined.

"I was so sorry to hear about this. I know Gran stopped by, but if there is anything I can do…" I began.

She bit into a scone. "These are good."

"I'll tell Gran. I've named a smoothie in honor of the sheriff. I hope you don't mind." *Better that she hears that from me and not anyone else.*

She sipped her coffee. "Not at all. He liked your drink. I liked mine. It's all bad timing and people found out you were pulled over that night."

"Circumstances make people connect things." I shrugged it off.

"Exactly. You're newly back in town, got pulled over, served him a new concoction and he died. People. I'm sorry, would you like some water or something?" she offered.

"No, I'm fine. Thank you. Do they have any idea what happened? Maybe an accident with his medication?" I asked.

"You're so sweet to think it wasn't deliberate. I know it wasn't you. Well, I know he wasn't sleeping with you. Your Gran raised you better than to sleep with a married man, no matter how your mother acted—you've done Bea proud."

"Thank you. I didn't kill him or anything either. You think he was having an affair?" I asked.

"I know he was. At least one. No, I'm sure you didn't kill him. Over a warning or even a ticket. People are so silly and dramatic. There are much better reasons, reasons that would make someone do something drastic." She patted the couch.

A little white dog hopped up beside her and settled in Mrs. Monroe's lap.

"I'd never have imagined the sheriff would ever do anything like cheat on you. I'm sure you've told the deputies anyone you suspect. Will your kids be coming home for the funeral?" I asked.

"That's why we've had to delay. That and the testing. But a couple of days. It'll be in the papers tomorrow."

One of the kids was my age, working in Louisville, and the younger one was in college.

"It must be so hard to lose a parent so young," I said.

"You lost your parents much younger." Mrs. Monroe gently stroked the dog. "Luckily we have life insurance and the house is paid for. That other woman will get nothing."

"Did he know you knew about this other woman?" I asked.

She chuckled. "He threatened to leave me once a week."

"Why didn't he? Or was it all just to get your feathers ruffled?" I asked.

"I think part of him wanted to. I had my lawyer picked out and ready to take him for all I deserved. I raised the kids on my own because he worked all the time. I did all the school stuff, little league and all the wifely duties of an elected official and sheriff. Charity work. I cooked, cleaned and looked after his elderly parents as well as my own." She took a deep breath. "All that work is worth nothing today."

"You're right. You did so much for him. He wouldn't leave you really—he'd never win another election. People would turn colder than a banker's heart on him." I started to suspect Mrs. Monroe a bit.

"Of course he would've—once he was ready to retire. A younger woman without all that baggage or anything to hold over his head? I think he felt he needed to keep the family together until our youngest was out of college and had a place of his own. Ed didn't want to ruin their childhoods." She shook her head.

"I'm so sorry. Do you think the other woman is behind it?" I asked.

She smiled slyly. "I'd imagine so. They've been seeing each other for well over a decade and he never left me. She probably got fed up that he wouldn't ever and slipped him something lethal."

"But he was with you all Sunday afternoon, right?" I asked.

"Most of it. He always slipped out to meet a friend or take a call from a law enforcement buddy. Networking with troopers and local police...he always had an excuse to go mentor someone or talk to a retired officer. I gave up trying to figure out what was real and what was a lie. Except his sister being ill, but that's real. Her son Hank needed to vent and was handling a lot on his own." She toyed with the string of pearls around her neck. "I know it wasn't you."

"Could you mention that to the police? I feel like people are making me the easy target," I admitted.

"I did. They didn't find anything in your blender. They don't have any answers, so they're sitting on it. That's what cops do. Trust me, I was married to one for so long. If they don't know, they string it out. They keep digging, chasing clues and leads. They won't rule out a suspect without a full alibi or other proof. Just wait it out and hope something shows up or guilt gets at a person. Most of the time, they get it right."

"Thanks for the advice. At least the police have a solid lead with the other woman. I'll let you rest. If you need anything, Gran and I are happy to help," I offered again.

She waved it off. "Very kind, but I'll be just fine once that check clears. As long as it wasn't suicide, insurance pays out and I'm the sole beneficiary."

"I'm glad you won't have money concerns. You deserve it after all that unpaid work." I wasn't going to flip her into an enemy now. Imagining myself in her shoes, I'd feel stuck, betrayed and resentful too.

"Don't take it the wrong way. I loved my family. I'd do anything for my children. I loved helping with the church and people. I loved my husband. I meant my vows. When you find out your life is a lie because the man you love wants someone else — it degrades it. I was a virgin my first time with Eddie, only him. I was a good wife. I never once thought of another man and I'm pretty sure he's had more than one mistress."

"I'm so sorry." I spotted a box of tissues on the table behind her couch and got them for her.

"Thank you. It's important that you understand I never wanted him dead. I wanted him to be as loyal to me as I was to him. I tried everything a wife could. Counseling to lingerie." Mrs. Monroe blushed. "When you marry, you put your happiness in someone else's hands. They can destroy it. Be very careful if you ever marry, Belle."

"I will. I'm sorry I brought all of this up for you. I just didn't want you or anyone thinking I held a grudge over a traffic-stop warning."

"No, dear. Though I do wonder what you did to get a warning and not a ticket. Flash a little something?" She looked at my bosom.

I adjusted my blouse even though it wasn't exposing much of anything. "No, I'd never. I think I heard his phone ring, but it was probably another police call that was more important."

"Probably his mistress. What late-night calls do we have in Sweet Grove? We'd have heard about a break-in or a health emergency." She tilted her head.

She wasn't wrong. "Well, I promise, I've never flashed anything or anyone. Whoever called, I just got lucky."

"With any luck, I'll get a proper death certificate and can file the insurance paperwork. Funerals aren't cheap." She sighed. "Come on, angel, time for your medicine wrapped in cheese. He just loves cheese."

"I'll show myself out. Please call, for anything," I said.

"Thank you." She carried her pet back into what looked like the kitchen.

At least she had her little dog to keep her company until the kids made it home. I was a bit surprised they weren't here now. Like it or not, I had two suspects now. The wife and the mistress. Odds of an accidental death were looking far less likely.

Then again, what if the mistress was married? Her hubby...*crap.* I hated to gossip, but I needed to know who the other woman was.

Chapter Seven

"Things were busy today. Your smoothies were popular. And that new coffee machine. No one broke it," Gran said.

It was nice to be home, away from all the chitchat. She set the table as I dished up two heaping bowls of stew. Gran had taken her seat and her head bobbed forward a bit.

I touched her shoulder. "Gran."

She snorted herself awake. "I wasn't asleep."

I chuckled. "Sure. Eat up. Coffee, water, Coke?" I offered.

"Water." She waved.

"Iced tea?" I tossed in another option.

"That caffeine will keep me up." She went to the fridge for butter.

I poured two glasses of water and cut up some bread. Once everything was on the table, we both sat and ate.

"I told you that your business would be fine. The sheriff's death was natural or an accident." Gran held up her hand. "May he rest in peace."

"Yes. But they're still investigating. I hate the idea that people would get the wrong idea. His wife has an interesting theory." I stabbed a carrot to make sure it was mushy enough. I hated raw or hard carrots, but well-cooked ones were delicious.

"You and your carrots." Gran teased as if she'd read my mind. "What's this theory of the widow?"

"How fast she'd gone from the sheriff's wife to widow. It's terrifying how your whole life can change like that based on one person." I shook my head. "She thinks it's another woman. The sheriff was having an affair."

"Lola Baker." Gran tore off a piece of bread and dipped it into her stew. "I love this stew. That huge pot will feed us off and on for a week."

"I'll have to scrounge around the pantry and see if we have what we need to make chili next week. But what about Lola?" I asked.

"I can make cornbread! It never paid to make big pots of stuff for just me. I'd freeze some and forget it until I couldn't recognize it." Gran's smile beamed up from her toes.

"Lola Baker is in the choir," I said.

"Yeah, she's the assistant manager of the florist in town. You know, where they do the farmers' market. Nice enough woman. Divorced young, no kids and other women's husbands, it seems." Gran shook her head.

"You knew about her and the sheriff?" I asked.

"Annabelle, I don't gossip. People confide in me because I care and can keep a secret. With the trouble your mother gave me, they knew I didn't judge," Gran explained. "I'm sorry, dear."

"I understand what you meant. Lola…" I had a goal and it wasn't my mother. I wanted to know who'd killed the sheriff or if it was really an accident. We needed to prove it wasn't me or the diner. It had to be hurting their business a bit too.

Gran took another big bite and chewed thoughtfully. After a gulp of water, she glanced at the fridge. "We have ice cream, right?"

"Gran," I said.

"Okay, fine. I knew about them, but nothing specific. Lola always liked older and powerful men who spoiled her, but she never showed it. Modest home, drove a Chevy and shopped at the usual places. Nothing snobby about her. Some women love secrets, makes things exciting." Gran shook her head.

"Every dog should have a few fleas. Do you think she'd be pissed enough to poison the sheriff for not leaving his wife?" I asked.

"Dear, I don't know her that well. I'm not into flowers so I only go to the florist if someone close to me dies. But to always be the other woman…what woman wants that?" Gran asked.

I nodded slowly. "But what would she be if she killed him? Nothing. Unless he changed his will somehow, she gets nothing and no hope of anything. It doesn't make sense."

"Love rarely makes sense. Not that that is real love. Lust, more like it. Proper love doesn't make you chase or worry. The intentions are clear. It might not be smooth sailing all the time — men and women are different and both have their moods — but no games. No cheating. No having your cake and eating it too.

Imagine what those poor kids will think if they find out how their father treated their mother?" Gran focused on her eating.

I did think about it and ate quietly, before my stew was cold. I could very much sympathize with the sheriff's kids, but they were lucky truly. They'd had both parents growing up. The sacrifice Mrs. Monroe had made to stick with it made me admire her just a bit, even if she pampered her dog like a baby.

"You okay?" Gran asked.

I blinked. "Yes, sorry. I was just thinking. Who's in charge of the investigation of the sheriff's death without the sheriff?"

Gran wagged a finger at me. "I saw Gus in that uniform today. He was brought on and he looked very handsome in it."

I arched an eyebrow. "You noticed? Maybe he came in to impress you?"

She blushed and swatted my hand. "Four men sniffing around is enough. And they're just friends. But you're young."

"He'll find out soon enough how this town ranks young women. Lurlene will probably sink her claws into him soon," I teased.

"Please, that girl is so desperate, it's sad. The pastor or Gus — whomever. She just wants to define herself by getting married. I'm glad you're not like that." Gran finished her water and puttered to the sink to rinse her bowl. "Ice cream."

"I'll dish it out. You let Duke out and feed him." I finished my dinner and put the dishes in the dishwasher.

Duke whined at the smell of our dinner and I tossed him a cooked piece of stew meat while he waited for Gran.

"Don't you give a dog people food," Gran warned.

"Never." I put the rest of the stew in the fridge and opened the freezer. "Vanilla bean. Where's your double chocolate?"

"Chocolate isn't good for dogs," she said.

"Is vanilla?" I asked.

She shrugged.

"Give him treats, Gran. Not ice cream." I filled up a bowl for her and added a spoon.

"Hush. I'm going to sit in my recliner, watch my shows and enjoy my treat. Then I may fall asleep with my faithful puppy. You go have some fun." She swatted my arm.

"Gran, I have to be up early for work tomorrow too. I don't need to go out," I protested.

"If you want to solve the mystery of the sheriff's death, you won't do it here. Also, if you want to find a husband and beat Lurlene to a wedding and give me some great grandbabies, you won't do that sitting in your room, either. Go!" She wiggled that spoon at me like a magic wand.

"Fine. I'll go visit Katie." I grabbed my purse, not even stopping to check how I looked.

* * * *

I checked my makeup in the mirror of the truck before I went in. That was only polite, and I popped a mint just in case. That didn't mean I was desperate for a husband. I just didn't want to be caught with something in my teeth or sit at home with Gran all the time.

Too wild like my mother or too lame at home—I couldn't win, so I might as well spend time with my real friends.

Katie was behind the bar, and I went right for her and plopped on a stool. "Need any help?"

"You're not an employee, but probably," she reminded me. "How're things?"

"Good. Not as busy as you are here. It's packed," I said.

"Everyone is wondering who the *other* woman in the sheriff's life is," Katie explained.

I sat up straight and leaned over the bar. "They know about that? Who do they think it is?"

"I guess some deputy mentioned it from the interview. Small towns and small-town cops." Katie shook her head. "No one knows for sure. No one wants to think about that old sheriff with a beer gut with his wife, let alone anyone else."

One of Katie's brothers got her attention. "Trouble in the back, sis."

"Watch the bar?" Katie asked.

'Sure." I grabbed an apron while dashing around the bar. Once in place, I tucked my purse safely away then washed my hands before filling the bottom of a tall glass with lots of maraschino cherries. I picked up the soda gun and found the Diet Coke button.

"You look at home back there," Gus said.

"Heavens to Betsy!" Startled, I hit the button.

I let it go just as fast, but I'd gotten the bar and the new deputy. "Sorry." I handed him a bar towel.

He laughed. "I shouldn't startle a professional at work."

"I forgot ice anyway." I scooped ice into my glass. "What can I get you? On me of course, for the mess."

"Club soda is fine," Gus said.

"Oh, Belle, that's not how you call dibs on a man or mark him. Poor thing." Lurlene walked up, took the towel from Gus and dabbed at the wet spot on his chest.

Katie walked up behind me. "Well, Lurlene, she might hit you with the water button and enter you in a wet T-shirt contest, but we don't need to see your itty-bitty assets in a C cup bra stuffed full of damp Kleenex, now, do we?"

The laughs from around the bar made Lurlene turn bright red.

"I can drink at home cheaper," she said.

"Please do," Katie called.

Lurlene left to whistles and jokes.

"That was a bit mean. *What God has forgotten, we will stuff with cotton* is a nicer phrase," I said.

Katie glared at me. "You need to stand up for yourself a little more."

"I did make the mess." I pointed to Gus' shirt.

"Cutest mess all day. How about we dance to cover it up?" he asked.

"I'm working here, not just some bump on a log." I looked at Katie. "Go ahead. I've got this."

I wiped down the bar and felt awkward no one was leaving. She sighed as I carefully used the soda gun to fill my drink without making a mess.

"He meant you." Katie shooed me away.

"No, she's the catch." I hooked a thumb at Katie.

"I'm not getting into this fight. You owe me a dance, Ms. Baxter. I'll collect one day. Now how about that club soda?" he asked.

"Right. I'm all thumbs today." I grabbed a glass, poured the ice and filled it without making a mess.

"She's been sleuthing today." Katie shook her head.

"Maybe I should hire her?" Gus joked.

Katie and I shared a look.

"Katie," one of her brothers shouted from the door.

"Busy night. People think with a dead sheriff that it's the Purge out there. I'll be back." Katie nodded to me.

I put a straw in Gus' drink before setting it on a fresh coaster. "See, busy. Besides, you don't want to get paired up with me. People talk and small towns are the worst."

"Why would it be bad with you?" he asked.

"You'll hear about it sooner or later. Lurlene would be only too happy to tell you about my family," I said.

"Your grandmother is kind. Besides, I don't think one person should bear the bad reputation of someone else because they're family. Do you?" he asked.

"No, but troubles seem to run in families. Sins of the father and all that. Teen moms is a bad pattern. Alcoholics. We learn what we see."

"Mind if I change the topic?" he asked.

"Beer, please," said the lead singer as he slid in next to Gus.

"Tap or bottle?" I asked.

"Tap," he said.

I pulled the handle and filled the glass.

"Want to sit in tonight?" the singer asked Gus.

"No, thanks. I'm trying to mingle and get some information," Gus said.

Maybe he just wants to know what I found out with my sleuthing?

I set the beer down and marked the tab the band had running so Katie could settle up with them later. No doubt they got some drinks on the house.

"When do you go on?" I asked the singer.

"Not for half an hour. I better go check and make sure the rest of the band gets here. Musicians. Not reliable." He winked and slid from the stool into the crowd.

Gus sipped his drink. "You and he are friendly?"

I shook my head. "Bartending, like the coffee or smoothie bar, is about customer service. I don't want to hurt Katie's business. You wanted to change the subject?"

"Right. You were sleuthing?" he asked.

"No, not really. I went to visit the sheriff's widow and take her some scones. We got to talking. But you already know about the other woman. Katie said everyone is talking about it."

"Someone let it slip. Lou." Gus shook his head.

"Whoever is the next sheriff will have his hands full. I wonder if they'll have a special election?" I wondered aloud.

"Actually, they'll appoint someone to complete his term and have a regular election since it's under six months away," Gus replied.

"Rough way to start a new job. Do you know who the other woman is?" I asked.

"I'm not sure." Gus leaned and put his hand under my chin, tilting my head until I had to look him in the eye. My heart beat louder and jumped into my throat, but I swallowed it down. "But you do."

My skin tingled and I was about to tell all when Katie ran up.

"Sorry. Gus, can I get your official help?" Katie asked.

"Sure." Gus released

"Everything okay?" I asked trying to hide my blush.

"The sheriff's nephew came by, already having had enough to drink. I know it's grief so I don't want to get Hank arrested, but I need someone more official than a bouncer to get him to move on. His friend seems sober enough to drive, but the poor kid just wants to drink more." Katie shook her head.

"Good night. Duty calls." Gus took a sip of his club soda and followed Katie.

"Night." I felt like an idiot all the way around, but I did have a lead ahead of the police. A lead I wasn't sure would actually take things anywhere.

Now I had even more suspects, though. The widow, the girlfriend and the deputies... Most of them would want to move up and be sheriff. Would they really poison the sheriff to get there?

I didn't think so, but I'd never thought the sheriff would cheat on his wife. I heard Gran's voice telling me not to judge people. *Just the facts. No judgment until the truth is proven.* I could do that. Think of all the people Sheriff Monroe had put in jail—one of them could've approached the sheriff like they wanted to thank him or talk and slipped him the stuff. Right there we had a lot of suspects I couldn't track down.

I looked up and the lead singer was smirking at me as the band set up. Maybe he'd heard about my mom? I wasn't going to prove that easy—no matter how good he looked in those tight jeans.

Suddenly I wanted to spray my neck with cold water, but instead I just took a long drink of my cherry Diet Coke. I went about serving paying customers and filling orders from waitresses now that I wasn't chatting.

Tomorrow everyone would be saying I was flirting with Gus. Luckily, I'd be busy. I had the shop then choir practice in the afternoon. There, I could make friends with Lola innocently enough. She seemed so genuine and kind. I hoped she wasn't a killer on top of being a cheater.

My sweet little town wasn't so sweet anymore.

Chapter Eight

My hair was up in a ponytail, but I'd managed to get up and moving on time. Gran busied herself setting out the baked goods while my fingers fumbled a bit as I made the coffee.

"Don't forget, I'm going to the beauty shop soon. I have to look nice for the funeral tomorrow. Might be a slow day," Gran said.

"Slow day here, but I'm sure the beauty shop will be busy."

"Very. Do you want me to see if they can squeeze you in?"

"No, thanks, I'm fine. I just felt like a ponytail today," I said.

"Don't get lax about your appearance. It reflects on the effort we put into the business," Gran said.

"I know. That's the same message from college. Clean and neat in everything. This is better — you don't want a hair in a smoothie, do you?" I asked.

Gran frowned. "No, I suppose having your hair up is more flattering than a hair net."

"Exactly. The busier we get, the more it could happen, so this is a good look for work." It wasn't strictly necessary, but it made Gran relax.

Just then her four friends piled in, followed by most of the deputies working in Sweet Grove, including Gus. I suddenly felt bad for not dancing with him the night before.

Not about his feelings so much as I'd wanted to dance. He'd be great for Katie—a musician and he had that cowboy feel to him without all the accessories.

I wanted to spend time with a guy who didn't know all the gossip and nonsense about my parents that had been passed down to me somehow. However, that wasn't a good reason to spend time with someone. I needed to learn about him too. Life was just too hectic to focus on men at the moment.

But he'd know about my parents soon enough if he didn't already, and helping Katie was more important than a dance. She'd helped me plenty when I needed it.

"You seem a million miles away," Gus said.

"Sorry, what can I get you?" I asked.

He really did look good in his uniform. Something about it made his shoulders look even more broad and strong. Lou and Mike were along with him.

"Three breakfast specials. Two regular coffees. Extra shot in my coffee, please," Gus said.

I got started on the coffee as Gran refused to take the money Gus offered.

"I heard the sheriff's kids are in town," Lou commented.

"I'd hope so. Poor dears," Gran said.

"The nephew stopped by the Honey Buckle. He had to be turned away," I said.

Gus shook his head. "Grief makes people do foolish things. He didn't need to drink any more. I had a talk with him."

"The kids are demanding answers. The body got released for burial, but the tox screen is backed up. They took samples just in case, but we can't keep him on ice indefinitely. They embalmed him." Lou drummed his fingers uneasily on the counter.

I handed over the coffees. "It's good to have closure."

"Thanks." Gus handed out the coffees. "Better get to it."

Lou and Matt headed out of the door with their bear claw pastries and coffees. Gus lingered.

"Something else, Deputy?" I asked.

"You know who the girlfriend is?" He leaned a bit closer.

I lifted a shoulder slightly. "Mike will too soon. Small town."

Gus leaned in. "Mike wants to be interim sheriff. I do too and I think I can bring fresh eyes to this place."

"Fresh, but not as tapped-in as people who've lived here forever," I pointed out.

"You think I'm not qualified?" he asked.

"I didn't say that." I cleaned up some coffee grounds and wiped off the counter. "I'm not a tattle-tale. I don't have proof or first-hand knowledge. I'm sure the funeral will be enlightening."

"You shouldn't be doing police work," he said.

I gave him a sweet and innocent smile. "Who said I was? I paid a condolence call. People share things with bartenders and baristas. The wife should be more than willing to tell you."

Gus clenched his strong jaw then relaxed it. "Thanks for the coffee, Ms. Baxter. Mrs. Baxter."

"Goodbye, Deputy," Gran called.

Things were growing chillier, but I didn't know for sure that Lola was the other woman. Mrs. Monroe probably had enough proof and I had no reason to doubt her word, but Gran had given me Lola's name. I had to find out today for myself, if possible. Choir practice had never seemed so interesting.

* * * *

I brought pastries to choir practice, as was good manners. The women went crazy for them. Lola hung back and made herself a cup of tea.

"You okay?" I asked as I filled up my water bottle.

"Sure, just a scratchy throat. Maybe some tea with honey will help," she said.

"Smart. I'm sure you're super busy with the funeral tomorrow," I said.

Her face fell and showed her exhaustion. "The flower shop is swamped. I probably shouldn't have left. With my voice and all, I'm more useful there."

"The choir is singing tomorrow too. I'm playing during the service. It's so sad, I wonder what happened." I sighed.

"I'm sure the police will find out." She sipped her tea.

"Mrs. Monroe seemed sure there was another woman, but why would she hurt him? What would she have to gain?" I wondered aloud.

Lola turned to me and shot me a hateful look. "I never expected you to be nosing around in other people's dirty laundry. Your grandmother raised you better."

"Lola, I'm sorry. I'm not trying to accuse anyone of anything or get into dirty laundry. I'm trying to prove it wasn't any of the businesses being impacted by the investigation. They're still holding pots, pans, my blender and a pitcher as possible evidence. No one else got sick. If it's true, you should talk to the police and clear your name. Were you the only one?" I asked.

Lola rubbed her eyes. "How could you say that? Of course."

"Sorry. Gran always said if he'll cheat with you, he'll cheat on you. I never forgot that saying and I've heard a lot of them." I handed her a tissue.

She sniffed. "She's not wrong, but he swore that once the kids were out of the house, he'd tell her and settle things. He wanted to be with me, but he was good to his kids. Isn't that the right thing?"

"It sounds you could give him heaven and earth and he'd still want a tater patch in hell," I replied.

She pressed her lips tightly together. "Your grandmother would never approve of any sort of cheating. Such an old-fashioned woman, and you're just like her. Be glad your mother didn't take you with her. If she'd have raised you, you'd be dead in a ditch somewhere."

On most days, I was very glad my mom hadn't returned. That didn't mean I didn't miss her and wish I actually knew her. I'd only ever seen pictures of her and some home videos. The fact that Lola knew my mother better than I did knocked me for a loop.

"The kids and nephew are in town. You might want to give the cops your alibi or clear your name before they try to accuse you. If Mrs. Monroe hasn't named you, they might get her to." I patted her arm.

She sniffed and nodded. "What would I have to gain by killing him? I didn't want to lose him. His wife is a good woman, but she didn't make him happy. Divorce happens. This is a small southern town, but it's not the fifties."

"You think she did it?" I asked.

Lola dabbed her eyes and stood up a bit straighter. "Who else stood to benefit? Someone might've wanted his job, but what else? The house, insurance money and all of that…right to the widow. Unless he had another arrangement in his will, but we never talked about that. I didn't want this money. I just wanted him. Tomorrow I'll have to stand with the choir and keep myself together instead of falling apart."

"You can attend the viewing tonight," I suggested.

Lola's lips quivered. "I suppose I could, briefly. I don't want to upset the family."

"Do you have any family around?" I asked.

She shook her head. "I met him after I divorced my first husband. The sheriff stood up to my ex. He'd hit me a few times and wanted to stay married because he thought he had me scared. It was Eddie Monroe who made me feel safe and strong enough to walk away. My ex married someone else and moved away. I stayed here. I felt safe with Eddie in power. He was just a deputy back then and his kids were little."

"I was in the same grade as the older one, Eddie Junior," I shared.

"You were too young to know of my drama. Don't fall for a married man. It's nothing but heartache. Even if he's a good man," Lola advised.

I bit my tongue rather than wonder how good could he be if he actually had the affair? If their love was that strong, he could've divorced his wife, given Mrs. Monroe her share of things and shared custody of the kids. People did it all the time, even in a small town. It could work out if they put the kids first and went on with their lives.

Bottom line, Lola was hurt but still in love. She had nothing to gain from killing the sheriff. Maybe something would come to light, but so far it felt like a dead-end.

"Ladies," the pastor said.

"Coming," Lola replied with a big fake smile on her face.

Luke came over and it was just him and me.

"How's business?" he asked.

"Very good. Thanks, oh. I owe you a dinner." I felt stupid. A southern lady didn't offer a dinner and not extend a proper invitation. I was forgetting my small-town manners.

"No, no that's not what I meant. Your grandmother had me over for dinner as a welcome when I first arrived. I was hoping I could take you out to dinner," he offered.

"Oh, I'm not sure." My brain fumbled for polite words. Was he with Lurlene? I'd been crushing on Gus and that band leader was attractive. None of that was appropriate to say.

Luke nodded. "I understand."

"No, I wasn't sure you were unattached. A single young pastor is usually a big target for the eligible young ladies," I rambled.

"You're not eligible?" he asked.

I tilted my head. "We both know my history. My parents."

"Small town gossip is a shame," he said.

"Yes, but the truth is the truth." I folded my arms.

"And you shouldn't be ashamed of it. I wasn't suggesting that. You should be proud of who you are. That's all we get judged on," he said.

I frowned. "How new are you?

He laughed. "That's the only judgment that matters. People are always looking to downplay their own mistakes. About dinner. I'm not attached to anyone. I'm not asking you out of pity or anything else other than wanting to spend more time with you."

"I'd like that, but people will talk. A lot," I said.

He leaned in. "People talk no matter what you do. Avoiding life because of what-ifs only hurts you. We can do dinner in Nashville, fewer interruptions or eyes on us," he suggested.

"People will find out," I reminded.

"We could check out some other churches' use of piano and music. I have a friend who is networked with a small group of churches. They tape their choirs and try to keep things lively. It helps keep people coming in. We could see the tapes then have dinner before we head back," he said.

"That feels like a lie," I said.

"You're not interested in other churches' music?" he asked.

"I never really thought about it. I love music, so I guess if you want my input, sure. No one from the choir coming along?" I teased.

"That would mean I have to choose. We have a variety of voices but only one pianist. If you can't play it, we don't need to consider it," he replied.

"If you can get a better pianist, it won't offend me. Just let me know when you'd like to go and I'll make sure we don't do anything too challenging. Practice." I headed for the church.

Everyone was staring at me.

"Everything okay?" Lola asked.

"Fine. Pastor just wanted to make sure none of his new suggestions were too challenging for me. He knows you guys can sing anything but I'm just okay. I'm going to practice and go over the music so you don't get too bored," I answered.

"You're great," Lola said.

The woman nodded.

"And the Bible doesn't change but the message is always fresh when you need it," added Ms. Weaver.

"Thanks." I got settled at the piano and warmed up.

Was the pastor really interested in me or was I a charity work? Was I convenient? Was I good for making Lurlene or some other woman jealous? Why was I so suspicious of people?

Lola gave me an encouraging smile. Part of me was beginning to like her.

Then again, maybe Lola had gotten sick of coming second and decided to end her relationship with Eddie in a way that hurt more than just him? She couldn't divorce him, so she took him away from the people he loved and who loved him, sharing her pain?

A woman scorned…

* * * *

Gran and I walked up to Hodgkin's Funeral Home and Crematorium a polite thirty minutes after the viewing had begun. The nephew, Hank, paced at the back of the funeral home viewing room like he needed a cigarette.

I handed the tray of freshly baked cookies to one of the Hodgkin brothers, who were perpetually in proper suits and at the ready with smelling salts or a fresh hanky.

The room hadn't changed since the seventies, according to Gran. The wallpaper was a pale seafoam green and the carpet a darker green with paisley pattern. Rows of maroon upholstered chairs filled the room and a cross hung at the far end, above the casket.

The overwhelming fragrance of flowers hit me as I went from the back, where people lingered — like Lola, who didn't even glance in my direction — to the empty middle section. I felt like a little kid again, or as if I was caught in a time machine. I looked up at the fans that were running and the popcorn ceiling. Nothing had changed.

The room was huge, but it was their only viewing room. People were either an acquaintance who shifted to the back after paying the appropriate respects, or very close to the deceased either as friend or family, which put them in the first five rows. People knowing their place was just good manners.

Catching up with Gran in the line, I brushed off any cookie crumbs that might've gotten on my good black coat. I nearly bumped the big picture of Sheriff Monroe but caught myself.

"I signed the book for both of us," Gran said.

"Thanks." I looked around, but the vibe was tense and that was never good.

The widow sat with her kids in the front row and received the line of mourners filing past the casket. The kids looked stunned. Behind them was the sheriff's daughter-in-law and the grandkids, too little to really understand it all.

Gran checked the cards on the flowers and found ours without fondling them all. She nodded in approval.

We filed past the coffin and paused for a moment. The line behind us was long so we moved on and approached Mrs. Monroe.

"I'm so sorry, Bonnie. There are cookies in the back room. You make sure to have some and keep your strength up." Gran always knew what to say.

"Thank you so much for the flowers and the homemade everything." Bonnie hugged Gran.

Eddie Junior, who had been in my class, stood up and chatted with Gran. I repeated the kind words to Mrs. Monroe that she'd hear over and over. What else was there to say?

I moved over to Eddie. "I'm so sorry. Horrible reason for a reunion." I didn't know what else to say.

"I never thought Dad's death would be a mystery. He was a cop. Being shot or stabbed. Even a high-speed car chase or something. This is just weird."

I patted his arm. "Any way it happens, it's not easy."

"All I think about is my kids growing up without him," he replied.

I patted his arm. "They have their grandma and your stories about your dad."

"You're lucky, Belle. I never thought of you as lucky, but family can be tense and complicated sometimes." Eddie shook his head.

"Your mom is a strong woman. If there is anything I can do, let me know. Is everything as okay as you can hope for?"

He waved me off. "Sure. Just everyone has an opinion about burial or cremation. What to do with his clothes or books. Mom gets all the stuff and money, but she wants to get rid of a bunch of it right away. I don't blame her, but we're not ready to sort and purge his personal things yet."

"That is a bit cart before the horse. Everyone has their own timetable for grief. You could compromise — get a storage pod, I suppose, so it's out of the house, but you can go through it later to see if you want to keep some memories. You're smart not to rush it," I suggested.

"Maybe. Thanks. You're always so practical." He studied me for a moment.

Gran touched my elbow. "You're holding up the line."

"Sorry. Someone get the hook and yank me off." I followed Gran and tilted my head sympathetically to Eddie's wife. She seemed so occupied with the kids that she didn't even notice.

"Too much chatting," Gran whispered.

"He was one of the guys in high school who wasn't a jerk to me all the time. I wanted to be nice." I folded my arms.

She used the chair backs to help steady herself as she walked. "Let's grab a seat in the back. We're not family."

Mrs. Monroe wanting her husband's things out of the house so fast was odd. What was the rush? I knew about the affair, but if the kids didn't, then it would feel very off to them. I thought she would've been more sensitive to her kids' needs, at least.

We sat in the very last row and Gran puttered off to check on the cookie stock. Hank leaned on the back of the chair next to me and bit his nails.

"Why are you hanging back here? He was your uncle," I said to Hank.

"I know, but I was a bit of a troublemaker in the family. I don't want to upset the precious widow. She hates when I smell like smoke or like I've had a drink in honor of my uncle," Hank snapped then caught himself. "I'm sorry. I'm not handling this well."

I glanced at Lola at the other end of the row. She gave us a half nod of acknowledgment. Inspecting the people in the back section, I didn't peg any other women who I thought could be mistresses of the deceased.

Was Hank drunk? Did he have a falling-out with Eddie Junior? Did he argue with his uncle? Hank's mother was Eddie Monroe's sister and she was very ill. Maybe it was just the stress of all that being on Hank's shoulders and no more uncle to consult for guidance? I felt that with Gran and she wasn't ill.

Just then the deputies filed in in their dress uniforms. Some state troopers joined them. I found myself glancing at Gus too much. He looked very sharp, but this wasn't the time or the place for flirting. Even if the theme of the day was that 'life is short'.

Chapter Nine

One of Gran's friends minded the shop the next morning. Most of the town had been at the viewing the evening before, but many had to work during the funeral, with it being a Friday. I had no doubt they'd done that on purpose. But Saturdays could be busy as well, so it was hard to plan for a turnout.

I might've skipped the funeral if Gran had someone young to escort her. Her gentlemen friends were there, but they were all over seventy. Gran had trays of desserts to deliver as well — it was just courtesy, but she couldn't carry those. I didn't trust the old guys to not drop them either. If I wasn't so curious about who was behind the sheriff's death, I might've dropped stuff off and slipped away to the shop, but showing up was appreciated.

The church service went off without a hitch. No one would misbehave with the pastor in the room. I was at the piano and the choir performed well. Lola looked like a zombie who hadn't slept in days, but she sang along and didn't make a scene.

Mrs. Monroe shot Lola the side-eye more than once, but nothing could be done in the church. Lola was a loyal member of the choir, so they couldn't ask her to stay home without addressing the issue. *Awkward.*

But things got far more interesting once we were graveside. I wasn't stuck at the piano anymore but standing among the group of mourners helping Gran over the uneven grass.

Prayers were nice, of course, and people filed by the lowered coffin to drop flowers in. It was nothing fancy or special—the sheriff wasn't in the military—but the state troopers did send a group in dress uniforms to honor a fallen man of the law.

The other deputies were there as well. No one would do anything stupid with so many police officers around us. *Right?*

Then one man walked by the grave and something other than a flower went into the hole.

"Ew, he's peeing!" shouted one of Eddie Jr.'s kids.

The guy stopped and tried to sneak away.

Gus grabbed the guy out of line and hauled him away from the area.

Luckily, Gran and I were ahead of the splash zone. I was in a gray silk dress with a black jacket over it. Gran wore black slacks and a gray print blouse, a debate we'd had for half an hour. Slacks at a funeral weren't a problem for a lady if she was a senior citizen, but she didn't think of herself that way.

"How could anyone act like that?" Gran asked.

"He's lower than a snake's belly in a wagon rut." I shook my head in disbelief. Gus had the guy in a squad car.

"Who was that man?" Bonnie asked.

"Dad was a cop, Mom. He made plenty of enemies." Eddie Jr. stood beside her.

"I'll knock his teeth out, whoever he is," Hank whispered.

"None of that." The pastor stepped out from the crowd as the final group dropped their flowers. "So sorry for the interruption. The Monroe family thanks you for your attendance, thoughts, flowers, prayers and kind words. Our service is concluded. You're all welcome to the Monroe home for refreshments. See me if anyone needs the address."

"No one from Sweet Grove would act that way. That man is a stranger," Gran said.

We all headed for our cars and I passed by Gus. We exchanged a polite but knowing look—just getting through the day.

"Gran, grab a ride with your friends. I'll catch up," I said.

She waved.

"Everything okay?" I asked Gus.

The suspect was in the car. "Yeah, he was arrested by Monroe years back and got released a bit ago. We hadn't been able to track him down, but he found us. I'm going to take him in and question him. Mike and Lou knew Eddie much longer than I did. I'll handle this. Maybe the killer found us?"

I smiled. "I'm sure they appreciate it, but they may have been part of his arrest and know him. I'm sorry things have been so weird."

"Me too. I'm not trying to use you to find out this town's secrets. I like talking to you," he said.

"I believe you. I like talking to you as well. But I don't think Lola had anything to gain. No money, no nothing. She's the only girlfriend that I know of, but the only motive would be revenge on the fact that the sheriff didn't leave his wife. Whatever was done to him wasn't done in a rage. It just doesn't add up," I said.

"That's work for the police, not you. But I appreciate it. I found out about Lola on my own." Gus grinned.

"Good. I hope the tox screen comes back so you at least know what you're looking for," I said.

"I just didn't want you to think I was running off and being rude," Gus said.

"Of course not. You have a job to do. You're going to the police station? Good luck." I turned and headed for my car.

I shivered and felt off. That chat had almost felt like he was going to ask me out, but with all the people filing by, I doubted it. That would be unprofessional and very public, though talking police business with me probably was too.

I headed to my truck and found Lurlene leaning on the pastor's car and crying. It was an act to get his attention. She really needed to get a life or a career she cared about. Unless she and the sheriff had been closer than I'd thought…but I couldn't believe she'd be the other woman, ever.

Hopping in my truck, I ignored her antics and patiently followed the procession of vehicles.

Without Gran in the truck, I felt really alone. Odd, I'd never felt that in Atlanta. A big city made it seem normal to be alone for all sorts of reasons—like commutes. Here, I knew everyone but felt like I was a sad single.

Maybe I was just a little jealous of all the couples? Then there was the sheriff, who'd had a full family and still kept a woman on the side. I felt bad for Lola again.

She'd pinned her heart and hopes on a married man. *Foolish and sad.*

I'd never let myself do that, but I wouldn't be any less alone.

I parked blocks from the house since I had no trouble walking. The elderly of Sweet Grove showed up in force for every funeral and deserved the closer spots. As I got out of my truck, Hank was there puffing on a cigarette.

"Hi, Hank," I said.

"Hi. I'm sorry about yesterday. I'm not taking this well," he said.

"I understand. I'm really sorry about the sheriff. Your mom isn't well enough to make it?" I asked.

He shook his head and followed me as I rounded my truck. "She's got Alzheimer's and it's pretty advanced now. Leaving her bedroom at the assisted care home freaks her out so much they bring all her meals in to her. I thought I'd be burying her long before Uncle Eddie. That sounds awful to think about, but you never know with this disease. Then someone kills Eddie. Who would do this? And that pissing thing. I'd like to beat that guy black and blue."

"It was very rude of whoever did that, but beating him up won't solve anything. Gus took that guy to the station and I'm sure he's handling it." I opened the passenger side of my truck. "I hate to be the damsel in distress, but would you mind very much helping me with these?"

"Sure thing. Maybe I can do one thing right today?" Hank put out his cigarette and carried two big trays of dessert pastries. I carried a smaller batch for the family to keep for later.

"I appreciate cha," I said, using a local expression.

"Your grandmother is a nice lady. I got some coffee the other day. She made me take a muffin and told me to stop smoking."

I chuckled. "That's Gran, feeding everyone and giving out unsolicited advice. I know you have to get back to your mom, but make sure to get a coffee or smoothie for the road whenever you head back."

He nodded appreciatively.

I held the front door open as he carried the trays inside.

The house was packed. He set the trays down in the kitchen. "I'm going to go out for some more fresh air. Too stuffy in here."

"Thank you." I began removing the protective wrap before moving the goodies to the dessert area.

There was a full spread of sandwiches, salads and even soup courtesy of the ladies' church guild. Gran was a part of it, but it was understood that she'd bring desserts. It was her signature.

I found Gran with many of the other seniors, filling a plate. She waved me over.

"Nice spread. Did you chat with the deputy?" she asked.

"Sho' 'nuff. Just a bit about that horrible man. I guess the sheriff had put him in jail and he got out. I'm sure they had to check on a lot of those as suspects. Revenge is a strong motive." I sighed.

"How odd that he'd bother to show up and be offensive. Speaking ill of the dead is certainly bad enough, but disrespecting their grave is disgusting. The man is dead—why come here to do that and upset his family? Rude." Gran ladled some soup as something caught my eye out of the window.

There was Hank smoking, but Lola was outside too and talking with him. She really didn't belong here, of all places!

Part of me wanted to go out there and shoo her away before someone else saw her. But it wasn't my place.

"Oh no!" Gran dropped her soup.

The edge of her blouse had caught alight on the little can flame warmer under the tureen. Lou and I quickly smothered the tiny fire.

"Get some water on it." Lou led Gran to the sink.

"I should get her to the doctor." I took my eyes off her for a second and ruined her day.

"It's nothing. It's not that bad," Gran said.

"I'm a nurse. Let me see." A woman came over.

It was Eddie Jr.'s wife, wearing a black dress and black pumps. Her long hair was up in a twist.

"I'd forgotten you're a nurse. I'm so sorry to be trouble."

She waved off Gran's words, and, with Gran's arm under the cool faucet, she peeled off her blouse and checked her skin. "Not too bad. Let's get it cleaned and wrapped. You should see your doctor Monday."

Bonnie came in with all the commotion. "Use my bedroom at the end of the hall. There's a first aid kit in the closet."

"So sorry about this," I whispered to Bonnie.

"Things happen, no matter what you do. Treasure your grandmother," Bonnie replied.

"I will."

The nurse led the way. We got into the bedroom and closed the door. It blocked out all the low conversation noise and I felt better. The bedroom was appointed with gorgeous furniture and a cozy blanket and the walls done in a cream and tan combo.

"I should be the one apologizing. I'm so clumsy at times. I bake all the time, but I didn't notice the flame keeping the soup warm." Gran covered her face with her unharmed hand.

"It could happen to anyone. They should've had it in a crock pot. My kids could've grabbed that and it would've been much worse. You spared us that." The nurse brought over the first aid kit from the closet.

Gran patted her hand. "I'm sorry, dear. I've forgotten your name."

"Jenni. I'm glad for an excuse to escape the crowd. So many people and the kids aren't used to this. Nursing is what I know how to do." She spread antibiotic cream on the burn and wrapped gauze around it.

"How often should I change that?" I asked.

"After she bathes every day. Let it dry thoroughly. It's okay to let a little air get at it, but be sure to wash it gently when bathing, let dry then cover it thoroughly with antibiotic cream and a gauze wrap. That'll get you through until Monday and make an appointment with the doctor as soon as you can. By then he'll have a better idea how it's going to heal. Burns can be moody. Some get oozy and others are super dry. This is barely first degree, so not worth a trip to Urgent Care." Jenni checked that the dressing wouldn't come off easily. "She'll need pain meds."

"I don't like taking that stuff," Gran insisted.

"Gran. Don't tell me that this doesn't hurt," I said.

"I have some pain pills left from the last time the doctor pushed them on me. If I need them, I'll take them. I have plenty to get me through to Monday. We need to get back out there. This is so rude," she said.

"Hardly." Jenni put the kit back together and looked at me. "She'll need to drink plenty of water."

"Thank you. Okay, Gran, let's try this again. I'll make you a plate and you can sit with your guys."

"I'm not helpless," she insisted.

"You're hurt. Let people help you. Do you want the guys to make you a plate?" I asked.

"No," Gran grumbled.

I turned to Jenni. "If you need me to watch the kids while you eat, just let me know. I'm good with kids."

She sighed. "Thanks. You have your Gran and I have my kids. I just hope that Lola doesn't come in the house. We'll have World War Three then."

"Wait. You know about that?" I asked quietly.

"My father-in-law thought he was sneaky, but his wife isn't stupid or too quiet about it. I think she worried her sons would act that way, so she let them know what she thought of it and how he'd hurt her. No one speaks of it, of course, but Pandora's box was opened long ago. I won't tolerate cheating and my Eddie knows it." Jenni shook her head.

"Good for you. I'm sorry Eddie Jr. and you had to know about those things. No one should think less of their parents. They're human, but that's cruel to be put in the middle. Thanks again," Gran said.

"Gran and I would love a visit from the kids at the shop—if you have time," I suggested.

"Thanks. We'll see." Jenni put the kit away as I caught up to Gran.

She was sitting with her guys, who were fussing. Milan got her something to drink.

I filled a plate for her and one for me and joined them.

"No soup—I'll get it," Milan offered.

I took charge. "She needs to drink more water while her wrist heals."

Gran took a bite of potato salad. "Plenty of water. Also, we need to talk about the business, Belle."

"Okay, but this weekend you're resting. I'll bake and handle the shop," I said.

"We'll make sure she only sits and visits," Joe agreed.

At least I had helpers to entertain Gran while I picked up the work. Her harem of men wouldn't let her lift a finger. *How does she have four admirers and I'm all alone?* Life was a mystery.

Chapter Ten

"More butter," Gran instructed.

I added butter and stirred the batter. "We're seeing the doctor at nine in the morning," I reminded her.

"I know. I made an appointment with the lawyer at eleven." She puttered around the kitchen.

"The lawyer?" I'd planted the seed about retitling things, but now seemed to be a rough time to push the issue. It was appropriate, but sometimes pushing something when people were most sensitive about it backfired.

She tasted the batter. "Yes, we have to be practical. You were right. I'm getting old, and if something happens…even if I just break a hip and need to be in the hospital for a bit—you need to have the power to make decisions."

"Gran, it's not about age. It's about protecting you. You and Grandpa earned that social security. It's not like we're millionaires. If the shop has a decent year, you have to pay back some of your social security money? That could make things tight for you. It's not fair to lose what you paid in. If I'm the owner, you don't have to worry. You'll get your checks and can work however many hours you like as an employee. I know you'll share all your ideas and help with the baking, but if you don't feel great, you can rest."

"It's a good idea," she agreed.

She'd made my earlier suggestion *her* brilliant move. "Yes. And we'll make sure you have a will and all of that squared away."

"I already do," she replied. "The government isn't going to steal my money. Your changes will make the shop hugely successful."

I poured the batter into the pan. "Your faith only scares me a little."

"You just have to be very sure you want to stay. I wanted to give you more time," she said.

"Time?" I slid the pans into the oven.

She started to clean up silently.

"Don't get your bandage dirty." I helped clean and started on some muffins. "What do you mean, time?"

"If you didn't want to stay," she said softly.

"Gran." I wiped my hands on the kitchen towels covered in pictures of daisies. "I'm not flaking on you. I'm not running off like Mom. I grew up here. It's home."

She nodded and sniffed.

"I'm not Mom. This isn't about guilt, either. You took care of me and I'm taking care of you. That's what family does. That's what you taught me. Mom couldn't handle it. She wanted something else and I hope she found it, wherever she is." I hugged Gran's frail form. "You're stuck with me, okay?"

"Okay. But you need a husband. You deserve a family," Gran teased.

"Nice try." I squeezed her tight and let go. "I need a successful business first. Worst case, if the shop doesn't work out, we move to Atlanta. I have connections there and can get a job that'll make us comfortable."

"And I just sit at home?" she asked.

"There are senior social centers. Just like you and your four friends hanging out at the shop."

She set up the muffin tins, putting in the wrappers for the individual muffins. Her hopes were slipping.

"Gran, I don't want that. I prefer to be here. But I need a backup plan so that I know I can take care of you. Small businesses fail all the time and in small towns, one economic downturn and we're all pinching pennies." I could jump into a lecture on how entertainment and pleasure travel trips were the first things to go, along with eating out, when times grew hard, but it wouldn't change her outlook.

"Have faith. What did I drag you to church for all your life?" she asked.

I stopped and gathered my thoughts. "Sorry, I have faith in your baking and my drinks, but coffee shops are about franchises now. Huge corporations that put shops on every corner and drive small owners out of business. It happens to some. I believe it won't happen here, but I need you to know that if it does, we'll be okay."

She wagged a finger. "Set the timer so you don't burn the pastries."

I did as she ordered and went back to the muffins. Southern women communicated through food a lot, and I took the win. She hadn't flat-out refused.

* * * *

The doctor was chatty but patient with Gran. We had instructions for the burn.

"Any other problems, Bea?" the old, bald family doctor asked.

"I do. She's been a bit sleepy lately. I just wondered if any of her meds are causing that?" I asked.

"Age is causing it." Gran shook her head.

The doc chucked. "I'm sure it's some of both. You can time your meds before bed so they help you sleep instead of fighting them."

She flexed her fingers. "My arthritis is flaring up more. That might have something to do with my injury or working more now that Belle stirred things up."

"I see." He felt her joints. "Finger joints are already pretty inflamed, and the wrist might swell and you won't really notice it as much. Topical treatments work well and I want you using wrist supports at work. An Ace bandage if that's all you want, but see if it helps. We can also try another medication, but I want to see your hand healed first, since that's a different sort of pain and you'll be on pain meds for a few weeks."

"No, you know I don't like those things," she argued.

The doc shook his head. "When you're suffering, you're not healing. Only take them when you're in discomfort."

"We'll fill it and when you need it, you'll have them, Gran," I said.

"Can't I just use the topical stuff when I need it?" she asked.

"The topical stuff will help with arthritic inflammation, but you can't put it on an open wound. Take this for now and I'll see you in a week. We'll see how you're doing. Try the topical on your other wrist for now and we can tinker with your arthritis pills later. Okay?" he asked.

"You just want to see me again," Gran teased.

"Get the most out of your Medicare. Any other complaints? Eating well?" he asked.

She nodded. "With Belle back, I'm eating plenty and resting."

"Good. And you, Belle? Anything I can do?" he asked.

I shook my head. "Tell everyone my smoothies are good for their health?"

He chuckled. "Sneak in some extra veggies with all that fruit and I will. You seem stressed—you're sure you're okay?"

"I'm fine. Just worried about this murder. The sheriff. People thought I did it and now it's a long list of suspects. Everyone is walking on eggshells."

"Oh, I know. I had the deputies come in and ask about what the sheriff was taking. Asking questions about what might've been slipped into something. He's not allergic to anything and that reaction would've been obvious." The doc shook his head.

"No tox screen yet?" I asked.

Gran frowned. "Are you running for sheriff?"

"No, but if people were trying to blame me and my smoothie for it, I'd like to know what killed him. Having this lingering out there hurts our business. I know it sounds horrible to be so selfish, but we're working hard and we're innocent. If there is a murderer in town, I want him behind bars."

"No word yet, but that sort of thing takes much longer than it does on TV shows. I know the medical examiner who did the autopsy. I'll see if he'll give me the info. Just so we can rest easy? But we'll have to wait a bit more," he said.

Gran beamed with pride, as if her connections had solved the case.

"Thanks, doc," I said.

He handed us the scripts and left the room.

"I have to come back," she grumbled.

"It's okay. You need to take care of yourself. It's aging," I teased.

* * * *

A couple of hours later, we were at the lawyers to change things over.

"You want to sell the business to your granddaughter?" Mr. Blake asked.

"We're in business together, really. I have a lease on the space, and I'd still work there some, but it'll be her business." Gran waved her hand like she had a magic wand.

Mr. Blake frowned. "The lease is in the name of the business, so if the business changes hands, it'll be fine, but we might want to speak to the landlord and assure them it's just a family thing. How much do you think the business is worth?"

Gran frowned. "I have the tax reports, but I'm not going to charge her."

"Then it's a gift and you're paying tax on the gift." Mr. Blake sighed. "Send me over the last three years of tax statements and financials for the last six months to get an idea of the income."

"I'm not charging her," Gran repeated.

"Gran, it's okay. I have some money saved up. I can pay you, we put that money in a joint bank account and use it only in emergencies. That way it's available to both of us just in case," I explained.

"You can do that?" she asked.

"I write you the check, you can put it into any account that you want. If you want to put it in a joint account, we both have access to, you can. *If* you want. But then if you need it but you're in the hospital and can't get to it, I can. If you want to buy something, you can. That's not illegal?" I asked Mr. Blake.

"No, not at all. If you had other family members, I'd suggest letting someone else be the joint account holder, but we all know the situation here. As long as you trust each other, it's the best way to handle it. Then we have a clear bill of sale for the business — we don't want to it to get messy."

"We'll stop on the way home and set up a joint bank account so it's there whenever we need it. It's not a rush — we're just gathering info and figuring out how to go about this." I smiled at Mr. Blake.

He leaned forward. "Mrs. Baxter, you're very lucky. I wish everyone looked after their senior family members like your granddaughter is."

Gran said, "I know. I want her joint on the house too. And my car."

"Gran, you don't need to," I said.

"Mrs. Baxter, your will specifies Belle as your sole heir. Everything in your name will be hers. You don't need to retitle anything personal. The business, if you want her to control it now — that's why you need to do this," he explained.

"Fine. Then just this," Gran said.

"Just email me or drop copies of those forms by so I can get our accountant to look at them. We want a fair price that won't red-flag anything. The government is nothing but trouble for a small business," he said.

Gran smiled politely. "You'll have it today. Thanks."

"Thank you. I think it's a smart move," Blake replied.

He stood and opened the door for us as we left.

As we left the office, Mrs. Monroe walked out of the insurance agent office next door.

"Hello, Bonnie, everything okay?" Gran asked.

Mrs. Monroe nodded stiffly. "Just fine. I had hoped one of the kids could sit with me through all that insurance paperwork. But it's filed. The funeral bill has to be paid."

"It's all still in your name, right? That way you can pay off everything you need to and have a cushion in the bank. No squabbling with the kids?" I asked. "I'm sorry, that's prying. I just know how relieved I was that Grandpa left Gran safe without any surprises."

I was too young to remember it in real time but, later in life, that bank account from the insurance had saved us many times. Gran finally told me once how Grandpa had always thought Mom would show up one day out of the blue and realize her mistakes. He'd wanted her home so badly. He'd thought he'd failed her. Gran had worried he'd changed something on a work policy or his pension to go to Mom instead of her. She had no control over his work benefits.

"You're sweet, Belle. Yes, it was in my name, so no stress there. But I still have one child in college and that's not cheap." Mrs. Monroe took a deep breath and tucked a tissue into her purse.

"No, it's not. But there are scholarships and loans. Widows and orphans fund for law enforcement. You have options, if you're not too proud to reach out," Gran suggested.

Bonnie fingered her necklace nervously. "We'll see how it all shakes out once everything is settled. I might downsize the house, and that would help. The boys are out of it and it's just me and my little dog."

"We have to keep going, and in the South that means eating. Why don't I treat you two ladies to lunch?" I asked. "Gran is bored with just me all morning. We can run by the bank tomorrow morning."

Gran waved at me. "Yes please, Bonnie, come with us. I can't handle more appointments today. Don't forget, we're always around to sit with. Come to the shop after for dessert. Belle's muffins were perfect today."

"Oh yes, how is your wrist doing?" Bonnie asked.

Gran dove into a recap of her doctor's appointment. Hopefully it'd take Bonnie's mind off her troubles. We walked toward the diner a few doors down and I braced myself for a lot of widow talk.

In order to be a widow, a woman needed one thing I lacked…a husband. I was pretty sure that would come up too. I ordered sweet teas all around and studied the menu.

I wondered what Gus was up to today and immediately squelched the thought. I had bigger fruit to blend than flirting with deputies. My business and a murder mattered more than having a man on my arm.

Chapter Eleven

Gran and I returned from the bank with a new account, plus the new water bottles included for opening a new account, which made her happy. Her entourage were minding the store.

"Thank you, boys, so much," Gran said.

"I'd say breakfast was on the house, but it always is," I teased.

Milan stood up and refilled his coffee. "We're happy to pay if you like."

"Belle, really," Gran scolded.

"It was a joke." I felt bad, but they were *always* there.

As I put on my apron, I reminded myself of the senior center we'd talked about in Atlanta. Here it was on her terms. No one else made up her social calendar or told her when to do what.

I only nudged a bit.

I poured myself some coffee and fired up the blender. It was amazing how people were using smoothies for a quick lunch. I'd never expected it, but I was ready for the rush. I'd added more veggies to the base and disclosed some of the ingredients so people felt healthier about it. The menu was only a one-page flyer, and there was a special treat smoothie every week that had chocolate or caramel in it for those wanting to splurge.

Lou and Mike walked in, looking a bit confused.

"Morning, Deputies," I said.

"What can we get you?" Gran asked.

"How's your hand, Mrs. B?" Lou asked.

"Fine, Lou." She patted his arm. "You look like you need some coffee."

He nodded.

"What's your poison?" I asked out of habit. "Darn. Sorry."

Mike laughed. "Actually, I needed that. It's too soon, but I know you meant well."

"It was a throwback to my Starbucks days, really, and I could only say that to my regulars. The menu was so full that it spellbound newbies," I explained.

"Give me a large iced dark roast with two shots of mocha," Mike said.

"Blond roast but five caramel," Lou said.

"Iced or hot, Lou?" I asked.

"Iced, please." Lou grabbed a chair.

"What is it? Did you find the killer?" I asked.

Mike shook his head and dropped a ten into the tip jar. "Gus is interim sheriff."

"Oh, well, I'm sure that's because he doesn't know people here as well as both of you. It makes him more impartial for the investigation of the old sheriff's death." Gran rambled a bit but she knew how to hop on the best version of news.

The men shook their heads and started chatting amongst themselves.

"Now Gus will be a prime suspect, but not his own," Lou said.

"Gus had no motive," I said.

"We all wanted to be the next sheriff, but he was so new. He'd have no loyalty to Ed." Mike shook his head.

I sighed. "Not years of loyalty like you guys, but is a hasty promotion worth killing for? With no guarantee it'd be him? I can't imagine. Just like I'd never hurt anyone because I was pulled over. People are grasping at straws. You and Lou would both be suspects as well, then. You'd be hoping to be the next sheriff. Interim is appointed but elections take time. All of you have time to campaign," I pointed out.

"I always thought the sheriff should be appointed by the mayor, not elected by the people. How do we know what we need in a good sheriff?" asked Freddie, the quietest of Gran's men.

I hung back as they debated the pros and cons.

"We should get back," Lou said.

"Why? We've got every right to take our full break." Mike sat down.

"Honey butter scone?" Gran offered.

Just then a line of people poured in, the pre-lunch rush for those on more flexible schedules. I was getting the feel for this place and it seemed like things might work out...if only we had no more murders!

* * * *

Gran and Duke were out like lights, watching a cooking competition show, so I left a note that I was going to Katie's. I locked all the doors behind me and all the appliances were off. I still felt bad, but Gran had always been a morning person. I just wasn't ready for bed at nine o'clock.

I drove, observing the speed limit because now I was paranoid that everyone was judging my driving. They all knew about that late-night traffic stop and that, apparently, I was a lead foot. Silly, but people wouldn't let stuff go. If I was outright speeding, I'd hear about it for a week.

The bar was packed, so I parked around back next to Katie's vehicle. It was usually reserved for staff, but I was close enough.

I went through the back door and found one of Katie's half-brothers making out with someone.

"Sorry. I heard you guys needed a hand at the bar," I said.

They didn't even stop to look up and her brothers were all so big and tall that I couldn't get a glimpse of the mystery lady. I wound my way through the kitchen and out into the bar area.

Katie and two other bartenders were working hard.

"Bar or tables?" I asked.

Katie looked like she could cry. "You read my mind."

"I'll take some tables. I need to stretch my legs," one of the bartenders offered.

I took her post. After tossing on an apron, I washed my hands and got to work.

"What's the big rush?" I asked Katie when I needed a bottle near her.

"Gus is sheriff. The whole town's talking about it." Katie winked.

"I heard this morning. My coffee and smoothie shop appears to be the morning watering hole and you've got the evening one," I said.

"Well, Gus is supposed be playing tonight with the band. Everyone is freaking out. Good for business. When the hot new sheriff is also a musician, the single girls go a little crazy," Katie teased.

"But why are people freaking out?"

"People want answers for the murder and our new sheriff is goofing off on a guitar," Lurlene said.

I smiled at her, despite every instinct in me. "No tox screen back, he can only do so much. Now that he's interim sheriff, it's a high-pressure situation?"

"It's not for you to decide, now, is it? You're just glad it's him so you're off the suspect list." She drummed her fingers on the bar.

"I was never really on it. Come on, think of all the people who Sheriff Monroe put into prison—those men have motive. He'd pulled over most of us at one time or another for a burned-out taillight or fooling around with a boy in the back of the car." I shot her a look. "But he got real criminals put in prison for years. Some of them must be out...that's who my money is on. If I were a betting girl."

Lurlene blushed a bit. "At least you're winning so far, betting on Gus." She stopped herself. "I'm...I'm thirsty. Can I get a rum and Coke, please?"

"Sure. I'm not betting on or after Gus. He's nice and doesn't have a list of prejudices against me, which is refreshing, but I'm sure you'll tell him all about it when it suits you. Right now, I'm not focused on landing a husband." I mixed her drink and set it in front of her. "If you want the pastor, you're going to have to be a bit more direct but also less clingy."

Lurlene furrowed her brow at me as she sipped her drink.

"Fine." I moved over to serve a group of men, who all wanted beers on tap. When I looked back, Lurlene's glass was just ice.

"Another?" I asked.

She nodded. "How can I be more and less?"

"Don't let your mouth overload your tail. I'm trying to help," I said.

"Explain." She squared her shoulders like we were in debate club.

I mixed her second drink and set it down. "Less clingy is obvious. You're doing the easily impressed wilting female thing. I get it, trying to make him feel like a big strong man. The problem is, he's a pastor."

"I'm aware." She glared at me.

"Well, a pastor's wife has to deal with a lot and she can't be bragging on all that she does. People calling you up at all hours of the night for help. Who does everyone go to in an emergency? The pastor or the mayor. That means you'd have to put people up if there's a house fire. Cook if someone can't. Take a casserole to every funeral in town. Help run all those charities and go to all the events. Reach out to people who are unemployed or struggling. I know the events part you'll like and the charities too, but you need to be sure you want that all for your life. People just expect it of you and it's a lot of work. Then, if you're sure, you have to show him you can handle all of those things, even things you might not like, with compassion and a real smile. People can tell when you're fake. We've known you forever," I warned.

"I'm not fake. I don't want to run the town shelter, and who would want to be woken up at two in the morning?" she asked.

"If someone was hurt, without a place to stay, or something like that—and you've got a safe warm house? A pastor's wife should want to help. You need to think about your man of interest. There are plenty of other targets. With the pastor, you have to be more of a help to him, more direct about taking some of the stuff on to help, and less needy. People don't want to hear about how much she does or how hard it is. Get on board with the Christian generosity or, otherwise, you'll make a terrible pastor's wife." I neatened up behind the bar as she drained her glass again. "Another?"

She shook her head. "Water, please. You know, I don't remember you having that bartending certificate thingy you have to in order to legally dispense alcohol. Maybe I should tell Gus about that when he gets here?"

Katie cut in like a drunk groomsman at a wedding. "You have sixty-some days to get it, once hired. She's not even permanently hired yet. Any complaints about the drink?"

"No," Lurlene said with a smile.

"Good. Quit stirring up trouble or I'll have one of my brothers take you home," Katie warned. "Belle, you might want to apply for that permit just to cover our butts. It's only a five-hour class."

"Will do." I pulled out my phone and added it to my 'do when I get a second' list.

When I looked up, Gus was sitting next to Lurlene. She was eyeing him like fresh meat.

Maybe my well-intended advice was a bad idea?

"Belle, hey. Can I get a water with lime?" Gus asked.

"Sure thing. I hear congratulations are in order, Sheriff. You're playing tonight?" I teased.

"I am, just a guest. Everyone knows then?" he asked.

"Small town." Lurlene leaned in. "My offer still stands to help you get the lay of the land."

"Thanks, I think I'm good," Gus replied.

"Too bad you're not married, Gus. The sheriff's wife does a lot of charity things. Raises money to help the policemen's funds, plans the policemen's ball, and even helps with the firemen's events — the fire chief isn't married. Lots of public events and helping the town." I poured the drink and stirred the pot a bit myself.

Lurlene was smart and knew this town as well as I did. But she was also desperate for something that was her own. She'd set her sights on a husband like her mom and granny had had before her. The world was different now, even in a tiny backwoods town. She was jealous that I'd gotten out.

Coming back was a choice and Lurlene didn't have many of those.

"No, no wife. We'll see if I get elected next year or if I'm run out of town on a rail," he joked.

Lurlene shot me a cruel look.

The lead singer came over and chatted with Gus for a bit, with their backs to the bar so I couldn't hear them.

"You just want me miserable," Lurlene said.

I frowned. "I really don't. The right guy isn't whatever guy turns up next."

She slapped money on the bar. "Good night."

"Lurlene, wait," I said.

"What?" she asked.

I leaned over. "I get working in the family business isn't great fun. You can still do something *you* want to do. There aren't a ton of choices here, but it's what you make of it."

"You want me to run off to the city like you, so you have less competition?" she asked.

"Life isn't a competition, but if it's what you want...go to the city. Or go to beauty school — maybe take a nail tech course, then work at the salon. You always look perfect. Why not at least help others look their best? Do something *you* like."

She stared at me for a minute, trying to think up a good comeback. "I do like makeup and nails. I did the makeup for my sister and her entire wedding party. That's pressure."

"If you like that more than working for your dad, it's worth looking into the cost of beauty school. You'd have to take a test with the state, just like me to serve alcohol. No big deal," I added.

"Then someone else can take my job at the store. Someone maybe who needs the work," she said.

I nodded. "Everyone wins and maybe your workday is more fun?"

"Thanks. I think," she muttered.

"Are you okay to drive? How many did you have before me?" I asked.

"None." She shook her head.

The lead singer saved me from an awkward talk. "Pretty lady, you can't leave before I perform."

Lurlene blushed and looked around.

"You are who I'm singing to tonight, so you have to stay." He kissed her cheek. "Want to help me set up?"

Lurlene grinned like the cat that ate the canary and followed the singer to the stage.

"Tell him I appreciate that, please," I said to Gus.

"Sure enough. You know she hates you." He smirked.

I scrunched my nose. "Good southern girls don't hate anyone. It's against our upbringing and etiquette, but it's mutual. Just keep an eye on her. Don't let him get out of hand or let her drive home while she's still buzzed."

"It's my duty as your sheriff." He winked.

"Watch that too. Don't get too smug or you're suspect number one," I warned.

"I've knocked you off the list for sure. Also, I've cleared my deputies. The coffin-pissing criminal had an alibi—he wasn't in town when the poisoning could've occurred." Gus sighed.

I shrugged. "I'm still at wife or girlfriend, but neither strikes me as evil enough. In all those years, if they didn't make a move then—why now? Unless one of the kids harbors a grudge about the affair, and they do know, then maybe one of them? The daughter-in-law is a nurse, so maybe she had access to some sort of drug."

He made a note on his phone. "I'm also looking into other released criminals that Monroe put away who held a grudge."

"Smart. I guess in reality it's someone obvious, isn't it?" I asked.

"Usually, but people can hide their motives well. Everyone has secrets. Plus, who *you'd* lay blame on in a certain situation might not be who someone else would blame. It's only obvious once you know the whole story." Gus looked over at the dancefloor as the song changed from fast to slow. "Come on, let's dance before it gets busy again."

"It's busy because everyone knows you'll be here tonight playing. I have to tend the bar." I put my palms on the bar like I was holding my ground.

He winked. "Come on. One dance."

"Go." Katie shooed me away.

I didn't even bother taking off my apron before I was on the dance floor, wrapped in his muscled arms. It was heaven, yet such a terrible temptation. I knew people were looking, so I didn't lean in too far. The music was too loud to talk, but that only made it better. The other senses took over and I felt safe in his arms.

The room was hot, yet I had the chills when the dance was over.

"Murderer!" someone shouted.

That sent a different sort of chill down my back.

But who was the shout directed at?

"Thanks for the dance." I headed back to the bar.

"Drunk idiots come with the territory," Katie reminded me.

"That's why I sell coffee. Sober idiots need more and more to function after you're done with them, but I never have to worry if it's safe to let them drive home." I went back to work, helping my friend.

Out of the corner of my eye, I saw Hank slipping from the back into the crowd and heading for the door. That was odd — maybe he'd stopped in because of Gus? I wanted to follow him, but I couldn't bail on Katie. Then I saw Katie's brother, the one who had been in the back. Was Hank his make-out buddy?

Chapter Twelve

Gran fussed as we sat in the room, waiting for the doctor. "I'm fine."

"I know. But the doc wanted to check your wrist and talk about your meds," I reminded her.

"We need to be at the shop, not running around appointments all the time. We don't both need to be here," she replied.

"It'll make me feel better."

The doctor knocked and shuffled in. "Morning, ladies, sorry I'm running a tad late. The detailed blood work came in on our late sheriff."

"And?" I asked.

The doc wagged a finger at me.

"Well, if it clears something up…that'd be great," I added innocently.

The doc opened Gran's file and sat down. "Nothing except the killer probably liked that show *Breaking Bad*."

"What show?" Gran asked.

"You didn't watch it. It was about making meth and selling drugs," I explained.

"You watched it?" Gran frowned.

"A guy I was seeing in Atlanta liked it." I couldn't tell her I enjoyed that violent a show or she'd be worried. Mostly I liked the crime-solving shows, but it had been intriguing. "Lily of the valley?"

"Don't change the subject to gardening. You were talking about meth and drugs. The sheriff wouldn't take those," Gran said.

I bit my lower lip for a moment to keep from hypothesizing too much. "It's relevant, I promise."

The doc sighed. "It takes a lot to kill someone. You'd want to mask the taste with something stronger. He wasn't ill the day or so before, so it wasn't a buildup. Honestly, your mint julep smoothie would've been a good choice."

"But I don't have access to that plant. Gran doesn't have a garden, just some flower boxes," said.

"No lily of the valley there. I prefer mums," Gran replied.

"Plenty of people have big gardens and it's a common plant. There's a garden walk every summer," the doc said. "I'm sure someone has plenty of it. Plenty of people probably don't even know they have it and that's the thing. So many plants are poisonous, if only people knew how easy it would be to get away with murder."

"It couldn't be accidental," I said.

"No, there are berries, but eating just a few would make you feel sick. Enough to kill a man the sheriff's size quickly without time for medical intervention would take a lot mixed into something he liked eating.

But it's in the cops' hands to find whoever had it around and had motive."

"Thanks, doc," I said.

"Now, Bea. How's the sleeping going?"

"I'm sleepier now with those pain pills. I'm fine, just check on the wrist and let's get out of here." Gran held out her wrist.

The doc undid the bandage and looked it over. "Very nice. Healing well. Okay, if your arthritis is acting up a lot or you're feeling too sleepy with that med, I want you to come back and we'll find something else. I know side effects make it hard, but we can find a balance that works for you."

Leaving the doctor's office, I saw there was a bit of an argument happening on the sidewalk.

"Why can't we park here?" the lead singer of Snakebite demanded.

"Park yes, you can't stay here two days," Deputy Lou replied. "We've got a trailer park with hookups on the outskirts of town."

"We just come in for a day or two to play. We can't afford the overnight fees," he said, then caught my eye. "Hey, Katie's friend."

"Dillon, right?" I asked.

"Katie talks about me?" He grinned.

"Her name is Belle," Gran cut in.

"Belle," Dillon repeated. "Yes, ma'am. You are?"

Where are my manners? "Sorry, Dillon and his band Snakebite. They play at Katie's bar. This is my grandmother, Mrs. Baxter."

Gran shook hands with the long-haired guy in town jeans and a tank top showing off a few tattoos. He was very polite.

"Mrs. Baxter. Sorry for the annoyance, but I'm just trying to find a place to park. We're from Kentucky and try to keep our costs down," Dillon admitted.

Gran's eyes narrowed. "Well, it doesn't belong on Main Street. People need to park and see to cross the street. But that trailer park is full of families and it's meant for more permanent residents. They don't want a band coming in all hours of day there."

"Where else do you think, Mrs. B.?" Lou asked.

"They seem respectful enough," Gran replied, looking at me.

I shrugged. "Katie's brothers would've kicked them out if they weren't playing nice."

Gran sighed. "They can park on my property."

I tried to hide my shock. "That's really nice, Gran."

"It is. You're sure, ma'am?" Dillon asked.

"My late husband and I have five acres. He used to ranch goats in addition to his day job. I sold off the goats when he passed. I've been thinking about doing something with the land again. I don't want to sell it off, but I want the land to earn its keep. Maybe goats, maybe horses. But a start is letting other people on my property," she said.

"What's the fee?" Dillon asked.

Gran looked at the RV. "Just run the fence and make sure it's solid. Clean up the land of any debris."

I pressed my lips together. "Gran, they're musicians, not ranchers."

"No, it's good. Physical labor we've got, keeps us in shape. It might take a lot of overnights to clear five acres," he said.

"I understand. No parties on my property, no fireworks, no leaving beer or any litter around. No girls knocking on my door looking for a phone or a ride," Gran warned.

He grinned. "We'll behave. Plenty of other places to party. If we're playing Sweet Grove, it's the music."

"When did we become mini-Nashville?" Gran asked.

I shook my head. "No idea. Maybe he likes Katie?" I teased.

Dillon folded his arms. "Katie is great. She runs a good place. I try not to mix business and personal stuff."

"Smart." Gran pointed at Lou. "Can you show the boys to my property?"

"Yes, ma'am, but are you sure?" Lou asked.

"It's my property. I have the room. There's water and septic hookups on the south side of the house. My late husband had a brother who RV'd all over the country and visited in the summers. Might need some cobwebs kicked out, but you boys can handle it." She wagged her finger.

"Thanks, Mrs. Baxter," Dillon called.

"We need to get back to work," I said.

"See you later." Gran waved.

"That was very nice of you. I really don't know those men," I said.

"Charity takes many forms. Sometimes opportunities to be kind pop up. I sort of miss the goats," she said.

I followed her, watching for traffic. Gran was livelier than I'd seen her in years. Musicians, goats or simply an expanded business—whatever it took, her life was going to be better.

* * * *

Back at the shop, Milan looked comfortable behind the counter. "The banana nut muffins were a huge hit, Belle. Got any more?"

"No, but thanks," I replied. "I'm open to suggestions for tomorrow."

"Belle, you have a visitor." Freddie pointed to a woman at a table by herself, staring at her phone.

"Trish? What are you doing here?" I asked as I went over.

"Oh, hi, Belle!" She stood up and hugged me. "Sorry to just drop in, but I have a job interview in Nashville in a couple hours and I thought I'd swing by here first since you're pretty close. I miss you," she said.

Trish was dressed to impress in a charcoal skirt suit and heels. Her jet-black hair was swept up in a twist, and she had perfect makeup and everything.

"You look great! I miss you too. There are really only a handful of people I miss from Atlanta but you're one." I heard the men mumbling. "Sorry. Where are my manners? Gran and her gaggle of men, this is Trish, a friend from where I worked in Atlanta. Trish, Gran and the gang."

"Hi," Trish said.

"Hello. What brings you to Tennessee?" Gran asked.

"A job interview in the city. If I get it, maybe I can see Belle more? They have multiple positions. I can ask if you can still get an interview." Trish nodded at me.

I shook my head. "Thanks so much for thinking of me. With friends like you, I don't feel so cut off from my old life. But I can't split my focus right now. If this is going to work, it needs my full attention."

"Nashville isn't that far away. People even commute from here. Everyone is so friendly." Trish shook her head.

"I know, small towns are like that. You're right, some people do commute, but not people with small businesses here and no one else to look after relatives that might need something at the drop of a hat. It's mostly the dad going into the city and a lot of moms work around here, so if the kid gets sick or hurt…unless they have a grandparent close by and are able to… It's just very complicated," I explained.

"The family obligation expectation here is higher." Trish sipped her coffee. "Well, if I get the job, I'll let you know. That way you have an in if you're looking for something. The pay is good and full benefits. You'll have to get something for self-employed people and that costs money. I know you, of anyone, can make this work, but you're giving up a lot of security and free time."

"I'm aware. But it's home. I really appreciate cha stopping by and thinking of me. If things go sideways, I'll be bugging you. Did you get a muffin?" I asked.

"No, I'm fine with coffee. I need to hit the ladies' room and get on the road. I don't want to be late looking for a building. You know me, worst sense of direction in the south. I can have the map on my phone and I'll get turned around." She laughed.

I pointed her in the right direction. "Ladies' room is on the side of the counters down that hall."

"Thanks." She headed there.

I walked over to Gran.

"She seems nice, except for trying to steal you away." Gran pouted.

"I'm not going anywhere. She's a good friend for keeping in touch and coming out of her way. Never burn bridges to good friends from the past." I tidied up some of the tables out of habit rather than lack of cleanliness. "Besides, she might get us some catering orders? Maybe your preserves will be stocked in fancy B&Bs or elite hotels because of her recommendation."

Gran sat back. "Maybe."

I grabbed a paper bag with nice handles from the back and added a small jar of each of the preserve flavors we stocked plus two biscuits and some packages of crackers that people used to sample the flavors.

Dashing to the back, I poured her a smoothie from the pitcher in the fridge into a to-go cup with a straw. When Trish emerged from the back, I had it all ready on the counter.

"What's this?" Trish asked.

"Just a little road trip snack or thank you for coming all this way to visit. If you land at a big place in the city, you could have us provide pastries or stock Gran's famous preserves at the hotel restaurant or any B&B around. Homemade, nothing artificial, no preservatives," I said.

"You sound like a commercial. We're not beggars, Annabelle," Gran scolded.

Trish smirked. "Annabelle. Never heard anyone call you that. Thanks for the treats. If I have an opportunity to plug you or get you in anywhere, you know I will. Keep your options open."

"Explore all avenues, absolutely. Need a refill on the coffee?" I offered.

"I'm good. Thanks." She hugged me.

"Good luck!" I called.

"Nice to meet you," Gran called as Trish left.

"That was a nice surprise," I said.

"You'd really consider a job in the city?" Milan asked.

"Mind your business," Abe shot back.

"I'm not ruling anything out until we're so busy we know we're succeeding. She could be a great connection for getting the preserves out there," I reminded them.

"Very true. I don't have any business connections. Now I can get back to baking." Gran sat with her fellas.

"Of course you can, but I don't mind helping. I was thinking, we have a big oven in the back-kitchen area. We could do some of the baking here instead of at home. Or at least have some stuff to make here if we run out of one thing, like those muffins."

"Really? You want two places that might catch fire?" Abe asked softly.

Gran playfully smacked Abe's arm.

I frowned. "Okay, maybe you're right. But we use the fridge and the sink here, so I'm sure the oven must work."

"It all works, but it's easier to mix up batter and bake at home. No distractions from customers like here." Gran shook her head. "You'll make this a full-service bakery."

"No, but I am thinking about something that might highlight your preserves so they sell even better." If I made it all about her, she'd jump on board.

"What's that?" Gran asked.

"Remember that sweet wheat or multigrain bread you made when I was little? It was great for sandwiches and you cut it thick. Toasted or not, it was delicious with butter or any of your preserves." I checked over my coffee machine and rinsed the perfectly clean-looking blender out of habit.

"I do remember that bread. It's a bit labor intensive but delicious. Why did I stop making it?" she asked more to herself.

"Once Grandpa was gone, I don't think you made it too much. It was his favorite. Only bread he'd touch." I paused at the good memories.

Gran sighed. "It hurt too much."

"Maybe I could try it here? If you have the recipe still...then it'd be fresh and the oven capacity here is just bigger."

"People won't come in for just bread and jam. I always have muffins or something else," Gran insisted.

"We can still do that. We'll have the coffee and the smoothies. But maybe, just maybe, that bread might be the key to inching us into the lunch market. Ham or turkey sandwiches on that bread with butter or mayo. Throw in a bag of chips and one of your homemade cookies for a quick boxed lunch on the best bread in the South." I'd been missing that bread since I was a kid and, for some reason, knowing there was an actual killer around, it made me want a simpler time and life.

In Atlanta, I'd always tuned out the number of murders or violent attacks reported on the news. Here, one was a major topic no one could escape.

"Belle? You okay?" Milan asked.

"Yeah, sorry, lost in memories," I replied.

"I think it's a fine idea. The diner is good, but people need a quick alternative," Joe added.

Gran smiled. "I think it's sweet that you remember that. Ham or turkey. Or ham and turkey. Swiss or provolone. Not *too* many options."

"If it goes over well, we can add a third sandwich — like egg salad or a BLT." I shrugged.

"Egg salad would please those vegans," Gran said.

I shook my head. "Vegetarians, yes. Vegans no. We'll see what sort of requests we get. Maybe put out a suggestion box?"

"I must say, I like you focused on the business and not on that murder. The deputies will figure it out now that they know about the lily of the valley," Gran said.

"The what?" her guys asked.

That would be their sole topic for the rest of the morning.

I went to work.

"Don't worry, dear. I have a friend who does the garden walk every day. I'll visit her this afternoon. I'll find the bread recipe this evening." Gran pointed in the air as if making a mental list.

"Good plan." She was so happy I couldn't be mad. She had the big scoop and liked the business ideas.

* * * *

That night Gran went to the diner with her fellas for dinner because I had a text from Katie insisting that I meet *her* for dinner. We needed to talk.

I was shocked she was letting someone else manage the bar.

I locked up the shop. Gran and the guys were already at the early bird special when Lou rolled by in his squad car and waved.

I waved back and rushed to the car. "Hey, Lou, any chance you're heading to the diner?"

"That was my dinner plan for tonight. Care to join me?" he asked.

I blushed. "Oh, no, sorry. I have plans with Katie, but not at the diner. Gran's there. I just wanted to know if you're headed there…maybe keep an eye on her and her friends? If she needs a ride home?"

Lou chuckled. "Sure thing. She's got a monopoly on the senior men in this town."

"She does, and I'm not asking why or how, but as long as she gets home safely, I'm grateful. If they stay out after dark…I'm not sure any of them should be driving in the dark," I said.

I should've asked the doc that.

"Don't worry. I'll keep an eye on her. You and Katie have a nice girls' night." Lou waved.

"Appreciate cha!" I called.

Did Lou really think I was going to ask him out?

I shuddered. He was more like a dopey brother.

I hopped in my truck and headed out of town. The steakhouse Katie wanted to meet at was just outside Nashville.

I made it and found her in a booth, looking shocked.

"You okay?" I asked.

"Sit. Order whatever you want. I'm paying." She sipped her drink.

The waitress came up and set down a coaster. "Can I get you something to drink?"

"I'll have a sweet tea like hers, and some lemon please," I said.

The waitress handed me a menu. "That's a Long Island."

"Oh, that's okay. Just a regular sweet tea for me, a couple lemons too. Thanks," I said.

"What's wrong?" I asked Katie as the waitress left. "Is it about the sheriff? I heard about the cause of death."

"Cause? No, it's not about the sheriff. Belle, I caught one of my brothers…in the back of the bar." Katie shook her head.

"Oh, kissing that someone? I saw it too and just slipped by when I came in the back door. I couldn't see who it was. They're grownups, Katie. Was it someone bad? Someone married?" I asked.

She shook her head.

"Someone underage? That's gross." I hoped I was wrong.

She shook her head.

I didn't want to suggest it was Hank, because I had no proof other than some awkward timing. It might turn out that Hank had gone in the back and spooked the couple, then the girl had gone out the back and Hank had left from the front. If they were trying to hide something, why wouldn't Hank go out the back?

"Did they do more than make out back there? I can see you wouldn't want to walk in on your brother and his girlfriend…that's some health code violations." I gestured with my hand to be polite.

Katie sighed and shook her head. "Let's talk about something else. The cause of death?"

"Lily of the valley. It'll be all over town tomorrow. I'm sure they'll drag Lola in for questioning." I perused the menu.

"You don't think she did it? Killed by a plant. She works at the florist." Katie sipped her drink.

"I don't think she had enough to gain to bother. You don't rage spike someone's food or drink with a poisonous plant. That takes time and research, or he'd have just gotten sick." I sat back as the waitress came with my tea.

We ordered food, but Katie looked more interested in drowning her sorrows.

"Was she some awful ex-girlfriend of his? A friend of yours? Oh no, a friend of your mom's. Some cougar?" I asked.

She rolled her eyes. "No."

"I'm sorry. I'm trying not to gossip, but you clearly can't stop thinking about it, so you might as well talk about it. Vent. Whenever you're ready. Until then, what do you think of Gus? He sort of keeps flirting with me, but I don't think he gets it. Why I'd be trouble for him to date," I said.

She scoffed. "Exactly. It's such a small town. If you were in Atlanta, no one would care if your mom was running around screwing a bunch of men and partying. The drugs could be a problem, but people aren't as judgy there. They mind their own business."

"It would be easier, but a lot more competition there too," I pointed out.

"It's so dumb. I always thought it was dumb, but that's just how small towns are. We're trash because of what our moms did." She shook her head.

"Sins of the father or mother. People don't really treat you differently...they just tend to bring up stuff that makes situations uncomfortable. Could've been worse. We didn't grow up in trailers." I sipped my beverage. "Oh, I get it — this girl is rich or from a perfect family so your brother will be treated like he's not good enough. Sorry. I skipped lunch. I need food."

"That's not the problem either. But we shouldn't have to accept that treatment. Rude comments or people thinking our family isn't good enough or unacceptable." She jabbed her straw into her drink.

"You can't change your family or other people. Moving to the city is your best bet if you're sick of dealing with this stuff. But it's expensive and stressful in its own way. Damned if you do and damned if you don't. You'll make some friends, but you can't rely on them, not like we rely on each other. Honestly, I'd rather put up with Lurlene and people like her than go back and feel like I'm always around strangers," I explained.

Katie folded her arms. "I get that part, but you did nothing wrong. You still get crap because your mom ran off and your dad was — well, no one knows who he was. That sucks for you, but it's not okay for people to judge you by their actions."

"Katie, we both know the facts of our lives and what people say. What does it have to do with your brother?" I asked.

She looked around. "I don't want them to suffer judgment."

"Okay, that's sweet of you, but you can't control others. I'll never judge him. I know you wouldn't. Is he dating someone to be concerned about? Was she in prison? Does she have a bunch of kids?" I asked. "Guessing games aren't my best area."

Katie leaned in. "It's not a she."

I pressed my lips together. There was one of her brothers who had never seemed flirty or into checking out girls.

"Okay. And that brother is the one with a really ignorant dad?" I asked.

"Yep. No wonder he's trying to hide it, but at my bar?"

"He does get breaks. That's his time," I teased. "He feels safe there. It's not about you."

Our food arrived and I dug in. She stared at her plate.

"Katie, do you have a problem with it or are you just worried for him?" I asked.

"I don't care, but..." She looked around as though people were watching.

The music in the restaurant was louder than she was. "It's okay," I said.

"Why wouldn't he tell me? Tell Mom?" Katie asked.

"He might not want people to know because of his dad. I don't think that will go over well. Is it a serious relationship? Who is the other guy?"

She shook her head. "The guy ran the other way and I didn't see. My brother said it was a hookup, and that it didn't matter. But he wouldn't say if it was the first time or the last."

"Katie, this is his deal. If he's not ready to talk about it to you or anyone else, leave him alone. I'd just ask him not to have any make-out sessions at work. Men, women or whatever...that's not the place to do that. Unless he's off the clock and in the bar like everyone else," I said.

"You're right." She took a deep breath and picked up her fork.

I tapped my knife on the plate for a second then stopped. *Nerves.* "Anyone else see them? I mean, if I did..."

"But you only saw my brother?" Katie asked.

"Right. I just wonder if he wanted to be caught." I shook my head. "I should focus on the sheriff's killer. That's a dangerous person."

Katie smiled. "At least a dozen people have lily of the valley growing all over their gardens. But it might help you narrow down the suspects with access. Gus doesn't seem to mind your help."

I chuckled. "He's nice, but I don't think it's a good idea, not if he wants to be elected sheriff on his own merits."

Chapter Thirteen

Biscuits and preserves with another option of double chocolate muffins were on tap the next morning.

"I can't believe I forgot to look for that recipe for my old sweet wheat bread. I bet I could do it from memory," Gran said.

"We'll find it or experiment. I'm sorry I was gone so long. Katie needed to talk and there are too many eager ears around here." I hadn't minded the fancy dinner complete with fudgy dessert.

"You girls deserve a nice chance to catch up that doesn't involve you tending bar for free. I hear how people gossip and eavesdrop," Gran said.

I smiled. "Her business is booming and bartenders aren't the most dependable. She has her brothers bouncing and doing security. You can count on family and friends far better than employees who aren't paid much and rely on tips. I know she pays better than some, but the professional servers go to Nashville and make way more."

"Most of the time, I bet that's true. She'll find her people. Just give her a chance," Gran encouraged. "I'm glad you're willing to help. Just watch out for rude men. Men today have no manners, especially when they drink too much. Even in a small town, they only behave when people are really watching."

"Katie's brothers are watching. I'm there to help and have a little friend time. You and your guys should come in," I teased.

She waved it off. "If I need a nip of something for a headache or a chest cold, I have it at home. Public drinking is only for toasting. That's what my grandmother said. One at weddings or funerals to honor the appropriate people — assuming those people drink."

I'd heard that rule a million times growing up. Some of the people in a small town like Sweet Grove never drank for religious reasons, so the crowds were always mixed. Some people drank freely, some socially and others not at all. *Why does life here always involve being penciled into a category?*

Men generally drank a lot more when their wives or moms weren't around. Grandpa often had a few beers with his buddies, but never at home.

It was more my fault than anything. They hadn't wanted to set a bad example — my mother had gone off the rails — so they'd led by example and given guidelines like that.

If Gus and I did go out, what would people say about me to him? About him dating me? It'd impact his running for sheriff. Lurlene would probably jump on him and steal him away in a blink.

I went into the prep area and cleaned the coffee machine for a new day. Then I headed into the back and checked what we had in the fridge, making a list of what we needed when we stopped off at the store later.

"Belle," Gran called from the front.

I went out and found Gus there. "Morning, Sheriff. What can I get you?"

"Coffee, two shots. Black. I'll have the biscuits and preserves today too. Thanks," Gus said. "You look busy today."

I worked on his order. "Busy means tired. But I was out with Katie last night. I heard about the lily of valley information too. Busy day."

He got himself some biscuits with the strawberry preserves.

"I had no doubt. Have you ruled out some suspects?" he asked.

I shrugged. "I never thought it was any of the deputies. Killing your boss to try and get the job is a dumb move. The kids weren't going to inherit anything. It was all going to their mom, so that's not really motive. Unless Eddie Jr. is annoyed about the affair—but annoyed enough to kill?"

"Wife or girlfriend?" Gus asked.

"The girlfriend worked in a flower shop. She could look up poisonous garden flowers and call it research for a customer who called. She could order it for the shop. But when I looked up the garden walk on the town website, her house hasn't been on it for the past five years. I don't think she had a proper garden, so work would be the only way to have a large supply." I handed him his coffee.

He handed over money.

"No," Gran called from across the room.

He put some money in the tip jar.

"That's a huge tip," I said.

"You're criticizing tips? You sound like a city girl," he teased.

I rolled my eyes. "They'd say it was too small. I'll just say thank you."

"What about the wife?" he asked.

I frowned. "She has a garden and her house is on the walk. Maybe she has it in her garden, but I don't see her getting her hands dirty and figuring out a way to get that much into her hubby. Unless she wanted to blame my smoothie... Maybe she saw an opening, but she was inheriting everything. Why rush and maybe get caught?" I asked.

"Unless she suspected he was leaving. I managed to get his phone records. Texts and all. The phone company wasn't the problem, but locating the phone was. His main one had been lost," Gus said.

"Main one?" I asked.

Gus sipped his coffee. "He had a family cell and a sheriff one. The sheriff one, we automatically had everything backed up and accessed. The family one, that was interesting."

He worked on his breakfast carefully so he didn't drip preserves on his shirt.

"You're teasing me." I set up the blender and prepped the area. It was early, but the breakfast rush would be rolling in soon.

"I shouldn't be telling you any of this," Gus said.

"I understand, Sheriff. The doc shouldn't have let the lily of the valley slip. I was just trying to help. Small towns have secrets and can be cold to newcomers. I have fresh eyes, but I'm one of them. A weird combo," I explained.

"You can't help it. You like solving problems. I see how you are, helping Katie. Helping your gran. You want to fix things. Make it better," he said.

"Maybe. But I'm not in law enforcement." I felt a *mind your own business, Miss Belle* scolding coming on.

"You're smart and you know this place. You are an asset, but you seem to avoid me. Why don't we go out to dinner and talk it over?" he asked.

I blushed. "If you want to be elected sheriff, that's probably not the best idea."

"I don't care about your reputation or whatever you think the problem is," he said.

"How can you say that without knowing what it is?"

He grabbed a napkin and wiped his fingers. He looked so strong and sharp in that uniform that I tried not to stare.

He cleared his throat. "I may have run a background check on you."

I frowned. "I'm not sure how I feel about that."

"You were so adamant, I thought maybe you'd had a wild youth," he replied.

I shook my head. "Sorry, I'm truly boring. Do you think the wife did it?"

Gus sighed. "Subtle subject change. I'm going to bring Lola in to talk to her because of the florist angle. Bonnie—well, she had no idea he was going to leave her. It was all over his texts with Lola though."

"Do you believe he was going to?" I asked.

Gus shook his head. "He was trying not to lose Lola. Unfortunately, I don't see another mistress on his phone to pursue."

"You wanted more suspects? Maybe Sheriff Monroe confided in his nephew? Like a guy-talk sort of thing?" I asked.

"I didn't see anything on the texts. Their phone calls were short and fairly routine weekly check-ins. I know Monroe cared about his nephew, but juggling women doesn't leave much time to look after your sick sister. He had longer chats with his sons. I might call them up and see," Gus replied.

"All the bank accounts, insurance policies and stuff went to his wife, so they'll still get their share. Whenever Bonnie passes, it'll probably be split. That's not motive, really," I said.

Gus sighed. "There was one bank account and an insurance policy benefitting the nephew, but he was caring for Eddie's ill sister... She had no one else, no other kids. Hank was just doing deliveries for a living so he could probably use the help with all those medical bills. Caring for his ill mother isn't a motive either. Hank might resent his mom. Heck, he might resent his cousins because they got to go off to college and move away. He might resent his uncle, but Eddie helped with his sister a lot, from what people say. Hank's dad ran off — that's not on Eddie. Hank couldn't blame his uncle. It'd be completely irrational. He didn't make her sick. Hank'd blame his father first, I'd expect. It's rough Hank couldn't go off to college and all that stuff with his mom so sick, but life happens."

"I can't argue with any of that. Family is complicated. But maybe it couldn't hurt to visit the sister and see how the relationship was between brother and sister first. Or talk to Hank without anyone around? See if he gets frustrated," I suggested.

"You'd make a good deputy," he teased.

I scoffed. "Not a chance."

Gran walked over. "Sheriff, would you like to come over to dinner tonight? I'm determined to entertain more."

"Gran, he's got a murder case," I said.

Gus ignored me. "I'd love to come over, Mrs. Baxter. Thank you."

"A man has to eat," Gran added.

"Sorry," I said as she walked away.

"Why? At least I know one of the Baxter women approves of me." He tossed his trash in the can, grabbed his coffee and headed for the door. "What time?"

"Six o'clock," Gran called.

"Gran," I said firmly once the door closed.

But more customers piled in for the morning rush. We were both hopping busy and moving product — it was a good sign.

That was a great thing, but I didn't have a chance to worry about dinner until after lunch.

* * * *

I changed my blouse four times. Gran had suggested a dress, but that looked like I was trying too hard.

"This isn't a date," I said to myself.

I'd touched up my makeup and fixed my hair. Refusing to fuss more, I went to help in the kitchen. Gran was checking the roast.

"What made you invite him?" I asked.

"Manners! He's new in town. He's a single man. The pastor isn't married, and with all the drama of the sheriff dying, I doubt they ever had Gus over. You'd be shocked what a good homemade dinner can do," she said.

I grabbed the bowel of potatoes and added cream before I fired up the handheld mixer. Once they were creamy, I turned it off, added butter and stirred by hand. "You know how this looks, right? It's like you're setting me up with him."

"Would that be so awful? I know your mother's stuff bothers you. If you get married to a good man and have a respectable family, it'll be easier. People will stop talking once they see what a good mother you'd be," she said.

I took a deep breath. "I know you mean well, but I'm not looking for marriage right now. I'm looking to get our business on the right track and make sure everyone knows it wasn't my smoothie that killed the sheriff."

"Oh, that'll be done in a month or two. You need to be thinking longer term, dear. I like your plans for the business, but you must have a personal life. Hanging out at the bar all the time won't help," Gran added.

I pulled biscuits out of the oven. "That's where everyone hangs out. I thought you didn't mind my helping Katie?"

Gran basted the roast and checked the carrots she had on the side. What was it with her and carrots? She served them as though they were as loved as potatoes or biscuits.

"I don't mind you helping Katie one little bit, but you know most of the people down there anyway. That's not a place to find a good man." Gran began to slice the roast.

I checked the time. Was Gus late? No, Gran was going to serve dinner at six p.m. on the dot. She hated tardiness.

"Gus is at the Honey Buckle regularly. He even sits in with a band Katie gets to play there. He's a guitarist." That might sour Gran on him.

"You both like music. Okay, that I accept. You're there to hear him play and to help Katie. He is there to play music. He comes to church every Sunday to hear you, and for God. Guitar isn't really good in a church." She shook her head.

I scrunched my nose. "I'm not sure if we resolved anything there or not, but you seem happier with that explanation."

"Let's see how dinner goes." She set the table.

The doorbell rang and Duke barked at the front door.

Gran shuffled behind me, but I caught the puppy by the collar before I opened the front door.

"Come in, Sheriff," Gran said.

Gus' face didn't look like he was ready for a night of fun and a home-cooked meal.

"I'm so sorry. I got a call. Someone has been going through people's gardens. No secrets in a small town. They also broke into the flower shop nursery. All the lily of the valley is disappearing." Gus rubbed his forehead.

"Sorry. Let me make you a to-go package," Gran said.

"I really can't wait. Rain check. Thank you, and I'm really truly sorry. The deputies are all at different scenes." Gus dashed off.

"It could be a clue. Good luck." I closed the door. Part of me wanted to join him, but I hadn't been invited along.

"Oh well, at least he showed up and we tried. Now we won't have to be so ladylike when we eat." Gran sighed and headed back to the kitchen.

I was disappointed and relieved at the same time. Men were so confusing.

"After we eat, we're ransacking this place for that bread recipe!" I announced.

Chapter Fourteen

After the morning rush, I was pacing in the back like a caged cat. I wanted to go out and find out more about what had happened. The vandalism of gardens had people annoyed.

I also had a list of ingredients I needed to get for Gran's bread. Checking the shop fridge, I added a couple of things we might need more of and double checked the space. We had plenty of it in the back. If we were paying the rent, we might as well use all the space and appliances.

I walked into the front and found Milan tinkering with my coffee machine.

"You need something?" I asked.

"The guys and I have been talking. If they're going to hang around so much, they can pitch in when things are busy. That way you're not here ten hours a day, seven days a week."

"I wouldn't say it's been ten hours." I wanted to downplay the stress.

"No, but it could be if we add lunch items beyond smoothies. If it works, you'll hire some part-time help, but until then, the guys can help a few hours here and there and not hurt their social security. A couple free hours at least to cover their coffee," Gran said.

There was no way I could argue with the. I smiled at the relief. "As long as they're willing to be trained my way and do it without cutting corners."

"No problem." Milan saluted.

"Cute. We can start after I get back from the store. But before the lunch rush, you can wipe down the tables and sweep the floors," I suggested.

"I feel like we're in the army again," Joe teased.

Gran giggled. "I'll supervise."

"Never doubted that." I headed out with a big list.

"One more thing, we need to do that grand re-opening next week. The lawyer called and we go over there tomorrow and sign the papers. Then you're the owner and I'm an employee. But I think we should have a reopening party here." Gran clapped her hands like a little kid.

"A party so soon?" I asked. "I was planning on it before the death."

"Well, free samples of new smoothie flavors. Maybe debut the new bread? Celebrate you and the ownership. People in a small town need an event, and with the death, it'd be nice to have something positive," she said.

"I guess enough time has passed. I wish we had the bad guy in jail. But we're not giving everything away," I warned her.

"No, of course not. Free samples usually lead to people buying jars of their favorite flavors. Now, you go shopping, but make sure you come up with a guest list. I'm thinking Saturday."

* * * *

I zoned out in the grocery store. Filling my cart and trying to think ahead, grabbing extra cleaning wipes and more dish soap. We'd found the recipe for the bread too late to make a batch at home, but I wanted to keep that to the shop anyway. With a full cart, I headed for the checkout.

I recognized the man ahead of me.

"Morning, Sheriff," I said.

Gus turned. "Belle, hi. Sorry again about last night. I promise, I had no fun."

"Everyone okay?" I asked.

"Yes. A lot of property damage. I'll update you at lunch. I'm heading over there now. I have to make it up to you," Gus said.

"No, we understand your work. Gran was pushy to put you on the spot with the invitation for the same night. You could've had a date or other plans." I made it sound like it was no big deal.

"Still, I'll bring lunch to you. I have a few calls I have to make before then." He took his two full bags and change from the cashier. "Thanks."

Martha waved. "Hey, stranger."

"Hi, Martha! How are you?" I asked.

I hadn't run into her since I'd been back and we hadn't kept in touch after high school. That was awkward, but Martha was sweet and friendly, still pretty and plump with dark hair that curled in big coils. I'd always loved her hair.

"Busy, what with working here and the twins. I don't know if you heard, I got married after one semester in cooking school." She rolled her eyes.

"That's great," I said without too much enthusiasm, as her face and words didn't match exactly in tone.

"I thought so too." She started ringing up my order. "I got my two girls out of it, but I should've finished school."

I opened my mouth but needed more context to say the right thing. "You can always go back. How old are the girls?"

"Five. So cute. Identical twins. But their dad. Not all military men are honorable. FYI, just so you know. I'm divorced now and a single mom. But how are you? I'm so glad you're back. I missed you." Martha totaled the order. "Let me just add a store coupon here."

"Thanks. Is your mom still a manager here?" I asked.

"She's too smart to give up a solid job, but she's mellowed a bit since my life went less than perfect." Martha blushed.

"At least you were married. I'm sure that made your mom happier." I slid my card into the reader.

"It plays better with the neighbors that I was married when I had the girls. But Mom was right. It hurts to say it. He was going to be deployed anyway, why not do school while he was gone? I thought I needed to learn the ropes of being a military wife and it wasn't for me."

"Love messes with your head, or so they say." I signed for my purchase.

I put the card away as the bagger put the many bags in my cart. I had to get back to the shop before Gus showed up with lunch.

"Hang on. You and the new sheriff?" Martha asked.

"Oh, no. Gran invited him to dinner. You know how she is with new people in town. The pastor's not married. The sheriff was killed. Gus started at an awkward time for the welcome wagon. Anyway, he got a call and had work to do. That's the life of a policeman."

Martha handed me the receipt. "He's not bad to look at. Just make sure you test him for a bit. That he's not a cheater and he's good with kids. Make sure before you walk down that aisle."

"Thanks for the tip, but I'm sure if we dated, everyone would be warning him about *my* family. If you like him, ask him out," I suggested.

She tilted her head and smiled wider. "Don't be silly. You're not your mom any more than I am mine. My mom had good taste in men. Everyone makes their own mistakes, but it's not some curse. My mom was talking about you being back and she was glad for Miss Bea. You've shown you're not the wild child your mom was. Don't let other people put you in a box."

I didn't mind chatting, since there was no one in line behind me. "Thanks. You know I know you wanted to be a chef, but you might want to think about being a teacher. Kids need to hear that sort of thing when they're young."

"I'm a mom first. Such a big job, but I'll think about things. I don't want to be stuck here forever—which sounds ungrateful, but I have more skills than this," she said.

"You do. You won every baking competition. There are always things to think about. Thanks, I gotta get back. See you around." I pushed my cart toward the door.

* * * *

Having the guys' help carrying stuff in was a huge plus. Gran and I put away the fridge items.

"Gus was at the store. He said something about coming by for lunch," I warned Gran.

"You better prep some smoothies then." Gran wagged a finger.

I frowned and went out to do just that. Training would have to wait until after lunch. But I could prep pitchers of the two flavors on offer today and have them ready in the fridge.

Gus walked in as I was cleaning up and Gran was teaching the guys how to work the cash register.

"Hope I'm not late," Gus said.

"No, what's with all the bags?" I asked.

He tilted his head to one side. "I told you I was bringing lunch."

"We were headed to the diner," Milan said.

"He didn't mean you. Come on. We're going to the diner. You two have a nice lunch," Gran said.

Then customers came in.

Gus sighed. "This was a bad idea."

"Having your own business is a lot. You can set up in the back, if you want. I'll pop in there when it's quiet," I offered.

When I had a lull, I snuck back and saw that he had enough options to make twenty sandwiches. The rolls were soft and I built a sandwich. Everything was fresh and that was nice.

"Thanks for lunch. What did you find out?" I asked.

Gus sat back from his food. "Last night? Bonnie's younger son had a lot of pent-up rage. He was so quiet at the funeral. Apparently, he hasn't been dealing with it at all. He went back to college—he's on a partial football scholarship so he had to go back and play to keep it. He got into fights with his teammates and was cutting class."

"Oh no. That's awful," I said.

"The school offered him counseling but he didn't show up. In the end, he got an incomplete for the semester and he'll go back next semester and retake those classes. His grief is too much. It's fair of the school, but he needs to handle his anger." Gus sipped a coffee.

"Was he the one messing up gardens?" I asked.

"Sure enough. He's sure someone killed his father and he's beyond pissed. He pulled out all the lily of the valley and broke every window in Lola's house. His mom had no idea he wasn't in school. I think he's been staying with Hank or another friend around town," Gus replied.

"Poor thing's madder than a wet hen. He definitely needs help," I said.

"He's in custody now. Destruction of property, threats and criminal trespass. He'd been drinking a lot. He wants answers and I don't blame him," Gus said.

"But ripping up people's gardens won't get the answers." I smiled and ate.

"Ideas?" Gus asked.

"Me? I don't know. It sounds like the son thinks it's Lola. Which means he didn't do it. The older son has two kids—there's no way he'd put himself in jail over his father's cheating. He has his own family to think about. Eddie Junior was more mature than most of the guys in school."

Gus sighed. "Wife or girlfriend? Poison is traditionally a woman's weapon. Bonnie seemed content to wait the affair out. Lola was pressing for a change and attention. She may have been plotting this for years and waiting for the time when she felt strong enough to issue an ultimatum. The youngest was out of the house, in college, and Eddie was close enough to retire if he wanted to. So she could've believed it wouldn't ruin his career if he just retired, divorced and moved in with her."

"You already brought her in for questioning?"

"She said she saw him for an hour that day. She could've fed him or baked him something and he ate it without thinking. He trusted her." Gus shook his head.

"He was cheating on his wife with the woman." I created an invite list on my phone while we ate.

"What are you working on now?" he asked.

"Just adding a few names to a guest list before I forget. Grand re-opening. I don't want to forget anyone. Might as well just ask the whole town," I joked.

"That sounds about right." Gus folded his arms. "I'm really sorry about last night. I was looking forward to it."

"Gran was too. You two make a cute couple, but you have some competition."

He laughed. "She was kind to invite me, but I've been trying to get you to dance with me. Spend more time with me," he said.

"You have too much on your plate and I have too much on mine right now. People will inform you soon enough about the type of girls you want to date," I said.

Gus smiled. "I know what I want, but I'm also very patient."

"Do you think email invitations are rude?" I asked.

"I'd just hang a sign in the window. If you have people out of town or who don't come in the shop, then maybe an email," he said.

"I think I want Hank to come. If he can get away. Taking care of someone is hard, but maybe he can bring his mom some treats. Cheer them both up?" I picked a couple of other friends from Atlanta, who I knew wouldn't make the trek, but I'd made the gesture and they knew what I was up to. I sent the email.

"You should set up an Insta for the shop too. Pics everywhere," he said.

"That's brilliant. I come home to Sweet Grove and I feel like I'm in a different time sometimes. I've been ignoring my social media horribly." I cleaned up the lunch and pecked him on the cheek.

"That was worth the suggestion," he said.

"Men." My phone binged.

"It's an email from Hank. *Sorry, can't make it. I have to work but I'll stop in another time. Thanks for thinking of me, Hank.*" I read the signature of his email. "Oh."

"What oh?" Gus asked.

"Guess where Hank works?" I asked Gus.

Gus shook his head. "We didn't dig into him that far. He's employed, no criminal record. Good relationship with his uncle."

"He delivers for a florist and nursery, a big one outside of Nashville." I sighed. "Something about that smells — and not like roses."

Chapter Fifteen

I found myself riding shotgun as Gus was on the radio, trying to figure some things out. Sheriff Monroe's son had torn up the town gardens and was in a holding cell, but we were off on a completely different lead.

"I saw Hank talking to Lola at the reception afterward, which I thought was weird," I admitted.

"We're pulling more info on Hank," Gus said.

I grabbed my phone and called Bonnie. "Hi, Bonnie, can I ask you a weird question?"

"Hello, Annabelle Baxter. Is that how you talk on the phone?" she replied.

"I'm sorry, I'm with Gus and we're trying to narrow down who killed the sheriff. It's important and I don't know how much time we have before we track down the suspect," I explained.

"What's your question?" she asked.

"I saw Lola and Hank talking to each other outside your house the day of the funeral. Is there any reason you can think of for those two to be nice to each other?" I asked.

"Nice? Unless she was asking him for money...no. I know he cashed in his inheritance quickly, but Lola might've tried to sweet talk him out of it." Bonnie sounded annoyed.

"Did you mind that your husband left some money to Hank?" I asked.

Bonnie chuckled. "No. Eddie helped as much as he could, but most of it fell on Hank to care for her. Hank will need that money to help if his mother hangs on in this state. She and I never got along wonderfully, so it was a load off my shoulders. Hank needed the help and he won't get any more of it. I have to look after my sons and grandkids."

"Did Hank get along with your boys?" I asked.

She sighed. "They weren't raised together. Hank was a mamma's boy. He didn't play sports or anything. He was an only child and smart enough. He should've at least been an EMT, but then he couldn't drop everything and check on her or take her to the doctor."

Bonnie was jealous that Hank doted on his mom and her sons had moved on to their own lives.

"At least we have our health. Do you know of Hank having any unsavory or dangerous friends?" I asked.

"No, he drinks a bit and helps friends by fixing up cars, because he has to fix his own car, but nothing bad. Is that all?" Bonnie asked.

"Yes. Thanks for the info, Bonnie. I'm sorry to bug you. I hope you can make the grand re-opening celebration. Bye." I hung up.

"Bonnie?" Gus asked.

"She's just jealous Hank takes care of his mom so much. No real help beyond that. Hank isn't impressive in his career or education. Of course, Bonnie isn't ill like Hank's mom. But why would he be chatting with Lola?" I wondered aloud.

Gus got a call. I couldn't hear the other side of it and all Gus did was grunt in acknowledgment.

"He's off work right now, so the GPS from his delivery truck won't help. His boss mentioned a bar he liked to go to with friends," Gus said.

"It's only barely three o'clock," I said.

"No accounting for what people need," he said.

"Why did you bring me?" I asked.

Gus sighed. "Sorry. I should've left you to your work. I just wanted to spend more time with you and we always seem to have issues."

"We're both working on our careers a lot right now. You need to solve a murder, prove yourself as sheriff and I am taking over Gran's business. It'll be in my name and everything, so that's pressure." I rubbed the back of my neck and tried not to think about it too much.

"You miss Atlanta?" he asked.

"Not really. I miss being invisible at times. Everywhere I go, it's a half an hour chat about what's happened since high school and how my family stuff doesn't really matter. Which means it still does, of course. Sweet Grove is so small and people don't forget anything." I shook my head.

"Martha was very chatty with you," he said.

"She was always nice. Her mom didn't like me. I just can't believe she has two little girls and an ex-husband. Katie has a bar. I feel so far behind," I admitted.

"You have a smoothie and preserves shop," he said.

I shook my head. "I'm buying it for cheap from my grandmother. I believe I can make it work, but it's her preserves and baking recipes. I need to keep an eye on her. I guess I can sympathize with Hank."

"But you suspect him," Gus said.

"Just because someone is good to part of their family doesn't mean they're all good. Maybe he got Lola a large quantity of lily of the valley from his job so no one would suspect her? His uncle was playing two women. Taking advantage of them. Hurting them. Hurting his kids. Maybe if he wasn't screwing around, the sheriff might've had more time to visit his sister or help his nephew a little more." I was trying to think about the emotional strain and resentment. "I don't have any siblings. I don't have parents to help out. Gran's health, safety and security are completely on me. That's a lot of pressure. Hank's mom got ill very young and is in the worst stages now. Gran is old and it's not a disease per se, but I don't feel like I'm ready."

Gus reached over and took my hand with his. "No one ever does."

"You?" I asked.

He shook his head. "I've seen it. So many times. People give up everything to take care of their family, and it's the right thing, but it drains them. Jobs don't care, employers don't understand and others, even others in the family, take it all for granted. Don't stop living, Belle."

"Thanks. That's why the business has to be my focus and it has to succeed."

"Thinking franchises already?" he teased.

His phone rang before I could reply. Gus answered and the voice on the other end was loud and muffled.

"Got it. Thanks." Gus ended the call.

"Interesting," he said.

"Interesting?" I asked. "You're a tease."

He sighed. "Hank was adopted. That makes it a bit more complicated. They were trying to get his birth certificate but hit a roadblock. It was a closed adoption."

"Adoption? No way. Hank looks like his uncle." I could see the similarities in how they stood, that little squint in the corner of their eyes and when they smiled really big, plus how their hair was curly and always cut short.

"He was adopted, no doubt about it. We'll get to the bottom of it," Gus assured me.

Adopted but looks like Eddie Monroe...

"Oh crap," I said. "Sheriff Monroe wasn't his *uncle*."

I grabbed my phone and called the keeper of Sweet Grove secrets. I put her on speaker phone.

"Yes, dear," Gran answered.

"Gran, is Hank really Monroe's nephew?" I asked.

"Of course, dear," Gran said sweetly.

"Gran, we know he was adopted by the sheriff's sister. Why?" I asked.

"That still makes him the sheriff's nephew. She wanted a baby. Poor thing never could find a husband. She looked like her brother and couldn't cook a lick." Gran clucked her tongue.

I almost joked that at least I could cook, but Gus was in the car.

"But Hank looks like the sheriff. He has a family resemblance. If he's not blood that doesn't make sense," I countered.

The line went quiet.

"Gran?" I asked.

"I'm having trouble hearing you, dear," she said.

"Gran, don't play games. Is Hank the child of Lola and the sheriff? Did they adopt him out to Eddie's sister to hush it up but keep him close?" I pressed.

Gus gave me a thumbs-up. Flaw found—he was a bit dorky at times, but still good-looking and hard-working.

"No! I can honestly say he is not the son of Lola and Eddie. Oh dear, I have customers. You go have fun on your date and I'll handle it. Don't worry about a thing about the shop," she said.

The call ended.

"She's good," Gus said.

"The best. Guilt bomb and skirting the truth. I'd bet she'd pass a polygraph with that."

"She would. You said Lola was a lifer in Sweet Grove. She grew up there?" he asked.

"Always in the flower shop and the choir. Divorced and no kids with the ex."

"People would remember if she left for some months to visit family then came back to hide an unacceptable pregnancy. Your Gran especially," Gus said.

"She would. You think she's lying?" I asked.

Gus shook his head. "I think Eddie had another girlfriend, at some point anyway. We didn't find any current *other* other women, but twenty years ago, who knows."

"Poor Hank," I said. *To be adopted by your aunt and forced to call her your mother and care for her while being denied by your true parents.*

"Poor Hank is a murderer. I don't think he helped Lola. I think he did it," Gus replied.

My phone beeped and I checked the message.

"Who's that?" Gus asked.

"None of your beeswax. Just a friend from Atlanta. Nothing to do with this case," I replied.

"A male friend?" Gus asked.

Gus is jealous? I shook my head. "No, Trish. She came by the shop to visit when she had an interview in Nashville. She got the job."

"Good for her," Gus replied.

"It is very good. She loved Gran's preserves. If she's working in a big fancy hotel, she can slip a jar to the restaurant manager to try. Or if things go south here, she might be able to get me a job that I could at least commute to rather than uproot Gran." I was very grateful for my friends and backup options. I had faith and would do anything for the shop, but the only sure things in life were death and taxes.

"Leaving us already?" Gus asked.

"Us? You're new in Sweet Grove. I'm old news and home. No, I'm not leaving, but we have to do what it takes. I'm not too uppity or pampered to not consider my options when I'm the only one to look after Gran," I shot back firmly.

He let the conversation lapse as he pulled up to the bar. It looked like the worst dive joint in a cheesy eighties movie about redneck roadhouses, right down to the Doberman Pinscher sitting outside—no leash, just a studded black collar.

Gus paused for a minute and seemed tense. He got on the police radio and let them know his location.

"You should stay here," he said.

"No way," I shot back.

He grabbed my arm. "Belle, I can't protect you if things go badly. If he's drunk and realizes we're on to him, he might run or fight. I don't want to wait for backup because someone will tip him off there's a cop car out here."

"They've probably already noticed. Go. I've been in bars before." I was a small-town girl, but I wasn't sheltered and clueless.

We got out of the car and went inside. Gus seemed tense, but he was on duty and things could go badly. Luckily, I'd taken a self-defense course while in Atlanta and I could always run for it.

He flashed his badge at the bartender. "Hank Monroe?"

I spotted him and went over. "Hi, Hank, sheriff wants to talk to you."

I wasn't an idiot. I kept enough distance between us so that he couldn't grab me, though I was pretty petite, no good for using as a human shield.

Hank frowned. "Why?"

"Your cousin tore up everyone's garden and broke Lola's windows," I said.

That wasn't a lie, and Gus might want to see if Hank knew anything. I hung back and listened.

Gus walked over. "Hank, come on, we need to talk."

Hank smirked at his buddies. "I don't feel like it."

"Sorry, not a choice." Gus grabbed Hank by the arm.

"Let go of me. I didn't do anything to Lola. She's innocent. You're trying to frame her because it's easy." Hank tried to pull away.

"No one is being framed. She's innocent, but someone did it." Gus slapped cuffs on Hank's wrist and twisted his other arm until he was cursing in pain.

Finally, both hands were cuffed behind Hank's back.

"Hey, Gus, I thought you moved," said a woman.

The redhead had a tray in her hand, wore a tight T-shirt advertising the bar and had leggings for pants that were so tight I didn't want to look anywhere near that area for fear the trim of her bikini line might actually be visible. Certainly, there were no panty lines. The hooker heels were overkill, in my opinion.

"Had some business blow through here. We'll be gone in a minute, Dina." Gus didn't even look at her.

The tension between them was higher than between Gus and Hank.

"Hang on," Dina said. She reached down her shirt between her assets and fished out a ring on a cheap chain. "Here. My new man said I shouldn't keep it or pawn it. He has real class."

"Fireman?" I asked.

"Mechanic," she said.

"Nice. I'm Belle." I would've shaken hands to be polite, but she'd just been wrist deep in her own cleavage.

"Dina. He's got a new girl already?" she asked.

"No, I'm just a friend of a victim, sort of. Trying to get a crime solved. Gotta train the new sheriff," I joked.

"Well, you tell the girls wherever he landed to steer clear. He's a handful, and not the good kind," she warned.

"Thanks for the info," I said. "We have to go."

Gus ignored our interaction. Dina stuffed the ring into his pocket and I headed for the door.

"I didn't help rip up any gardens," Hank insisted.

"Never said you did." Gus nudged Hank along and read him his rights.

Hank struggled getting in the back, but Gus managed it.

"I didn't touch the gardens. I'd never hurt Lola."

"Is she your birth mom?" I asked.

Hank froze and the car got very quiet.

Gus shook his head. "Wait until we're at the station. We need to record the interrogation."

"She's not," Hank said.

I looked back and his head hung in defeat.

"We know you're adopted. I don't blame you for being angry at your birth father. He was a good uncle, but that's not nearly enough to be a father." I caught his gaze.

He shoved himself back into the seat.

"He never took care of them. Any of them. He just cast them off if they were too much trouble," Hank replied.

"How many kids did he have?" I asked.

He shook his head. "I meant the mistresses. I'm the only bastard, as far as I know. Lola isn't my mom."

"Who is?" I asked.

"Birth mom? She died a few years back. Lung cancer. I couldn't take care of her the way I do my adopted mom. I swear, I wanted to tell everyone the truth about Eddie, but no one could know. Lola told me it'd be wrong to hurt my cousins. She found out about Uncle Eddie's history. I swear he only had his sister adopt me so she'd be taken care of by someone. He dumped me on her to get out of two obligations. I have two half-brothers who don't know I'm their half-brother. That's still a secret." He shook his head. "It's bad enough when no one wants you, but when they use you — put you close enough to watch but far enough away where they don't have to *really* care. Not like a father."

"I'm sorry," I said.

"What made you do it?" Gus asked.

Hank looked out of the window. "He told me he was going to cut Lola loose. She was demanding that he leave his wife. He said she made threats about telling people. Ruin his job or something else. I tried to calm her and told him to leave it. He started telling her he'd leave his wife again and she was okay."

"You were trying to help," I said.

He shrugged. "I wanted what family I had. Lola was nice to me. I love my mom, adopted mom. I do, but she's ill. She's not herself at all anymore and doesn't even know who I am. I don't want to upset her when I visit her. Lola let me vent and acted like a mom. Bonnie didn't want to be bothered with me. She treated me like the no-good nephew. It was fine — I wasn't hers. But he just kept using and hurting people."

"You put a stop to that," Gus said.

"I didn't plan it. It just came out," he said.

I turned to look at him but held my tongue.

"Out?" I asked. I bit my lower lip. "You got that much lily of the valley together on the spur of the moment?"

He shook his head. "It wasn't for him. I collected the berries of a bunch of poisonous plants. I crushed them, kept the juice just in case for Mom. I'd been gleaning from work for over a year. If she got too sick, she wanted a way out. Fast and certain death. I just couldn't do it."

"But she has Alzheimer's. Can she make that decision now?" I asked.

Gus looked at me. I couldn't fault her either.

Hank shook his head. "No. It'd be me making the call and I can't do it. I'm a coward. I've always been a coward."

"No one is saying your position was an easy one. Eddie should've helped more with that sister of his. But using that poison on him... How did you do it?" Gus asked.

Hank sighed. "Lola and I talked that day. I texted him that I wanted to talk about Mom. He came over after dinner. He was raving about that smoothie of yours, Belle."

"Thanks," I replied.

"I offered him coffee and I put it in there. He said it tasted funny. I told him it was a chicory blend. He drank it all and asked for a refill in his to-go mug. I was just glad he made it home."

"You just did it. Cold and planned? That's not you, Hank," I said.

Hank looked everywhere but at my face. A tear ran down his cheek.

"I told him it was wrong to cast off Lola. You don't dispose of family, no matter what. He said she wasn't family. That's when I asked if I really was his family or if, once Mom passed, he'd cut me loose." Hank sniffed.

"And?" Gus asked.

Hank shrugged. "He said I was a grown man. I was his nephew as long as I didn't upset his *real* family or embarrass him."

"Embarrass how?" I asked.

Hank shook his head. "Doesn't matter. I did it. For my mom, my birth mom, for my aunt or stepmother and for Lola."

"I don't believe you. You told him, didn't you?" I asked.

"Told him what?" Gus asked.

Hank looked down, but his face was bright red. "Nothing to tell."

"I saw you at the Honey Buckle. You came out of the back like you'd been caught. You were there making out with... It was you. I walked by," I said.

"I don't think anyone begrudges him having a girlfriend," Gus said.

Hank looked up. "It's not a girl. Sheriff's gay nephew. He said he'd rather I was dead."

"That's what made you do it," I said.

He looked down. "I told him I'd never say a word. I'd move away after Mom died. No one would know. He calmed down, I got him a whiskey and added the poison to that. Coffee was a lie. We drank to the new plan. He couldn't get out of my house fast enough after he had a good stiff drink. Like the sight of me made him sick."

"He was really sick and died shortly after getting home," Gus said.

"That man's selfishness had controlled so many lives for so long. He wasn't going to control me for another minute. I'd rather be in a literal prison than one of his making." Hank exhaled deeply and the tension seemed to ease away.

"I'm so sorry, Hank." I meant it. I was also sorry for Katie's brother.

"I know. You're a good one, Belle. I'm sorry you got any blame or suspicion on you." Hank nodded.

Sliding a look at Gus, I couldn't read his expression. We'd found the killer, but nothing was black or white.

"Get yourself a good lawyer, Hank. Juries are human—you tell your story. You're under arrest on suspicion of murder. The rest isn't up to me." Gus sighed.

I smiled slightly at him. If we could keep Gus, we had a good sheriff.

Epilogue

Dinner with the pastor was one thing I'd put off. Not out of wanting to get avoid it, but with so much going on with the funeral, Gran and solving a murder. Musical research for the church or a date wasn't my top priority. I kept my commitments to practice and service, but life in a small town proved far busier than I remembered.

We'd sat through an hour of videos, but dinner was the real event. There was no mistaking that. I freshened up in the ladies' room of a nice restaurant. I'd gone with a blue sundress. Not too formal but not too casual. I didn't regret it until he said Italian. Pasta sauce splattered on my dress showed how inelegant I could be at times.

I touched up my lipstick and added a bit of perfume. One last check of my phone to make sure Gran or her fellas hadn't texted, then I was done. I headed to our booth and settled in.

"Would you like some wine?" Luke asked.

I looked up from the menu. "No, thank you."

"You don't have to be extra anything because I'm a pastor," he said.

"I'm not. I have the grand reopening tomorrow. It'll be an early and very long day. I might have a glass of wine tomorrow night after all the work."

"Smart." He held up his hands in defeat. "I should've waited for this until after the reopening."

"No, it's been too long. I agreed to this and I was looking forward to it, but then so much happened. I appreciate your patience. I never planned to get so involved with..." I sighed.

"Gus?" he supplied.

"No, Gus and I are just friends right now. There may have been a flirtation, but I found out he just very recently broke off an engagement. He's a great sheriff and everyone has a past, but not everyone is upfront about it. I don't mean to gossip, but you deserve the truth about where things stand."

He put his hand on mine as I held the menu. "It's not gossip when it happens to you. But there is some stuff that people don't want to talk about early in a relationship. In those first couple of dates, it's seeing if you're compatible and have chemistry."

"Very true. Let's just have a nice dinner and find out if we want to do it again?" I suggested.

"Sounds wonderful," he said.

We ordered and talked about the music.

"I heard your grandmother was allowing a rock band to park on her property when they're in town?" Luke asked.

"She is. I was surprised but, you know, random acts of kindness... They're helping clean up the acreage. I think she's going to bring in goats." I chuckled.

"Goats?"

I nodded. "I remember when she sold them off. I cried. Baby goats are adorable, but she needed the money. They eat anything but they eat a lot of it."

"Sold for?" Luke asked with trepidation.

"Meat. I mean, the baby ones could go and be part of a dairy or petting zoo. Some people adopt them for pets now. Very different. A dairy with a petting zoo or adoption option would be the smart thing. Fancy cheese and milk—when the goats get a bit on in age, sell them off to a meat distributor. Goat is as good as beef."

Luke looked around. "You're lucky this isn't hardcore cattle country. Those could be fighting words," he teased.

I laughed. "True enough out west. Barbecue goat isn't a big business here, but there's a market. Cattle ranching would just be too much money, work and too big animals. We'd need staff. I think the goats we could get along, and have some teens from town coming in and feeding them, cleaning up a bit, and so on."

"They could run a dairy?" Luke asked.

I chuckled. "No, just to get started. That dairy thing is more of a pipe dream. Lots of equipment and trained staff. We're not in a position for that. But ranching goats for pets or dinner is feasible. Grandpa did it with no help and he worked a full-time job."

Luke grinned and tried to hide it.

"What?" I asked.

"You in that pretty blue dress, so proper playing the piano. I can't imagine you chasing around a goat pen all muddy."

"I've done my share of manual labor. Mucking goat pens or picking up after Gran's dogs. Cooking and baking are now just as menial to some. Where did the pride in service go?" I asked.

"The world is not what it used to be. That's why I'm grateful to be in a small town. Working with your hands is every bit as important as pushing papers or online businesses. If the world lost its power or Internet connection for a week, how would people live?"

"Don't tell me you like zombie and apocalyptic stuff?" I asked.

"It'd be slightly wrong for a pastor to admit, but considering the rapture potential and tribulation is all coming, preppers aren't all crazy. Some are, but not all," he said.

"That's another reason goats are smarter to ranch than cows."

He frowned and cocked his head. "Why?"

"Think about it. If you have your family or a small group, say fifteen people, and if you butcher a whole cow, it'll take a while to eat through all that meat. How do you refrigerate it?" I asked.

"A huge problem," he agreed.

"A goat is a smaller animal. You'll be able to use up the meat more efficiently without waste. Plus, they breed faster, have more than one kid at a time, and don't eat nearly as much as a cow." I sipped my water.

"What's your favorite zombie show?" he asked.

I grinned. The pastor's shining exterior had given way to actual interests and we had something more than music in common.

* * * *

The grand reopening was packed beyond my hopes. People enjoyed the smoothie samples and coffee drinks. The tension of murder was gone and now the truth was out.

"Oh, my, Belle, were you really there?" Martha had her two girls while her mom hung back a bit.

"I was. I got an email from Hank about how he couldn't make this and I didn't know he delivered for a nursery. It just clicked. He'd been hanging around Sweet Grove more than normal. I thought it was for his aunt, but…" I waved at the cute girls who had their mom's hair and big brown eyes. "Who are these cuties?"

"Bonnie had no use for Hank." Martha winked at me. "Glad you and Gus got the mean man. This is Melissa and Cecilia, better known as Missy and Cissy. Girls, this is my friend from high school, Belle."

"Like Belle from *Beauty and the Beast*?" Missy asked.

"It's spelled the same. Short for Annabelle," I said.

"They should've called you Ella, then you'd be a princess, like Cinderella," Cissy shouted.

"Belle is a princess and she has a library," Missy argued.

"Cinderella is better," Cissy sniped back.

"You know what, you two look like the princesses here. Would you help me test out a new smoothie? It's called the Princess Smoothie! Expert taste testers needed," I said.

The girls looked at each other, even putting their foreheads together. Then they turned and in unison said, "Okay."

"Don't let them be any trouble for your work," Martha's mom said.

"No trouble at all. It's new and it has to be just right," I said. "Can I get you something?" I looked at Martha and her mom.

"Just a coffee, plain," Martha's mom said.

"Martha?"

"I'll try one of those coffee iced flavored things," she said.

"Any flavor specifically?" I asked as I led the girls behind the counter and put them in stool high chairs. "Stay here. Your thrones need you."

The girls sat up straight. Martha stayed close on the other side to keep an eye on them.

"Hazelnut, if you have it," Martha said.

Gran laughed from behind the register. "She's got everything. Belle, the bread is cooling. Last batch in the oven."

"I can help, if you need it," Martha offered.

"Thanks. I think we have things under control for now," I replied.

Lurlene sauntered up to the counter. "This caramel mocha iced coffee is too much mocha and not enough caramel."

"Wicked witch," I heard Cissy whispered to her sister.

"Girls," Martha scolded.

I filled the blender with fruit and milk and a bit of food coloring to give it that popping princess pink. As I blended, Gran added caramel syrup to Lurlene's drink.

"If you want another one, I'll remake it," I offered.

Lurlene smiled politely. "No. I'm just more of a caramel girl, I guess."

"Let us know if needs more or you want a different one. We could make one just for you? The Caramel Bomb." I never said I was *good* at naming drinks.

"Like a cherry bomb." Martha laughed. *At least she got it.*

Katie and her brothers came in and I couldn't miss them.

Lurlene glanced over. "This is perfect. Thanks."

"You're welcome." I called. "Gran, Martha's mom needs a black coffee, plain, please."

"On it." Gran clapped her hands together.

I had a mix of fruits but added a bit of fruit punch flavoring for the kid's smoothies and blended it extra smooth. I started Martha's iced coffee while I was at it. Gran's guys were mainly on cleanup and stocking today with so many people out there. The preserves and muffins were flying off the shelves.

"You know what else you should sell? These little mason or preserve jars are adorable. Mason jar mugs for coffee and tea, and like cute little regular mugs with uplifting sayings. And those tumbler things for iced coffee or tea. Do you have sweet tea on the menu?" Martha asked.

"Don't tell people their business," Martha's mom scolded as she took her coffee from Gran.

"Those are great ideas, Martha. It'll cost a bit to stock the inventory, but if I can find a place to start small, there is room here for more shelves." I pointed to the walls that needed paintings or a little merch for display.

The beeping from the back made me stop. "Oven."

"I'll get it in a minute." Gran looked overwhelmed with the people.

"I can handle an industrial oven." Martha scooted back behind the counter. "Is that okay?"

"Martha, you're a lifesaver," I said.

"An hour late and I'm replaced." Katie made it to the counter.

"Never." I hugged her and whispered in her ear, "Please help Gran with the register. She's good, but slower than molasses in January."

Katie winked. "Gran, you need a break. I've got the register."

"No, you're our guest," Gran insisted.

"Gran, she came to help us like I help her at the bar," I called.

"Uncle Milan, Gran needs a break. Take her to the diner," Katie overruled.

"You girls just want to talk boys and have fun. I could use some air," Gran relented.

She got applause as she left.

"Boys are dumb," Missy said.

"Some of them definitely are," Katie agreed.

I poured their drinks into non-breakable glasses and grabbed the whipped cream. "Now the crowns."

I tried to get them as high as I could as the girls cheered. Then I added sprinkles and straws.

"Princesses, please taste your smoothies," I said.

Martha's mom had her cell phone out and recording. The girls sipped and dabbed their fingers in the whipped cream.

"Excellent!" Cissy declared.

Missy stuck her nose in the air. "I like purple better, but it tastes really good!"

"Color options. Good note. Purple, pink, rainbow?"

The girls grinned like Cheshire cats. "Yes!"

"Bright blue," Cissy suggested.

"Bright blue. Sounds like a plan. Now sit tight and enjoy, I have to check on the bread." I dashed in the back.

Martha had the bread out and cooling. "No more?"

"No, we're just testing it out. I made one batch yesterday and it wasn't perfect." I sliced a cooled loaf and added some butter. "The girls are adorable."

"You're good with them. Thanks." Martha cut her own slice. She tried it without butter. "That's really good!"

"Gran's recipe." I tried it. "That's the bread I remember from my childhood. Sandwiches might be a thing."

"And soup. With that bread, soup in the winter. That's a hit." Martha nodded.

"Gran and I can't do this alone. You wouldn't be looking to leave the grocery store, would you?" I asked.

"Work here?" she asked.

"I need someone here who can juggle customers, blend drinks, prep food and even handle the oven without getting overwhelmed. Gran and her guys run at a different pace and that's fine for most people – they can clean and restock and handle the slow periods. But the breakfast and lunch rush…no way. Plus in between the baking now, I'd need someone from, like, seven to three for sure. We bake the sweet stuff at home and are in early to prep," I said.

"Yes!" Martha burst out with a smile.

I frowned. "We haven't even talked salary. And I'd need you on weekends too."

"Working for my mom at the grocery store is… It's like I'm still a kid. I love her helping with my girls, but I feel like I'm constantly reminded I screwed up and it's a pity job. I can do this. The girls' dad gets them every other weekend. My mom never works weekends, so she can cover the others and they might drop in to visit, if that's okay?" she asked.

"Sure. I'm glad the girls see their dad," I said.

"Me too. He's only in Nashville so he rarely misses a visit. As long as you match what I'm making at the grocery store, I'm in. I'll start now," she offered.

"You already have and I appreciate it." I sliced up the rest of the cooled test loaves and put them in a basket. "Let's get them hooked on our bread."

Martha grabbed an apron, put it on, picked up another basket and filled it with the rest of the bread. "We'll need bread bags and ties to sell by the loaf."

"You're on top of things. I love it. Start a list of your ideas," I said. "Wait. We have to wait for Gran to get back to bring this out."

Martha nodded and put an empty basket over the bread to help keep it warm. We headed out and the girls, hopped up on sugar, were excited that their mom worked here now. The stink eye from Martha's mom was hard to ignore, but I sensed an undercurrent of pride.

Katie's brothers were in for the protein smoothies. Apparently, they lifted weights at a gym not far from her bar. One of them was decidedly avoiding eye contact with me, but I hadn't blabbed a single thing around town regarding him and Hank.

"Great shop, Belle," one of them said.

"We'll get out of the way now," another said.

They put some money in the tip jar.

"Thanks, guys!" I called.

"Did they pay?" I asked Katie.

"Naturally, but I think you need a punch card thing. Like, buy five fancy coffee drinks or smoothies and get the sixth one free."

"Or an app. Your own store app," Martha said.

"I appreciate cha both. The app might be too ambitious for right now unless we know someone who'll design and maintain it for free. Punch cards we can order along with business cards," I replied.

Martha groaned. "This hazelnut drink is heavenly. You need to put it in a frozen coffee form."

We had a tiny break from the rush and I mixed up a hazelnut frozen coffee drink while Katie showed Martha the ropes of the register.

Martha's mom came over. "I should take the girls to the park. Let them run off the energy."

"Thanks, Mom," Martha said.

She came over to me with a ten-dollar bill. "You didn't charge us."

"Martha works here now. She gets a family discount. The girls' drinks were my idea. It's on the house today." I waved off the money.

"Small businesses are risky, but you've got good products. And good workers. Thanks," she said.

"I only hire the best," I said. "Bye, Princesses Cissy and Missy."

The girls waved regally as they left the shop.

Gran and her men rejoined the party. "Bread time!" I said to Martha.

"On it." Martha dashed to the back and came out with the two baskets of bread.

"What's going on?" Gran asked.

"I hired Martha to help us. And your bread is ready. It's perfect." I let her try it first.

She gave me a thumbs-up with her mouth full.

"Everyone! There is a special treat. At least for me it is. When I was little, Gran made a homemade bread that was to die for. Sweet but not too sweet, it was perfect for jams or sandwiches. We found the old recipe and have been making some test loaves. Martha has the batches for you to take a piece and try. If you love it, we might put it on the menu where you can buy a loaf, or we could make sandwiches with it for lunches. Please do try it, and give us your feedback. There is a suggestion box with paper and pencils by the door. If you want more smoothie flavors, more coffee varieties, more jams or anything, let us know. If you don't suggest it, you get what you get and you don't pitch a fit!"

Gran laughed. "We're not trying to compete with the diner, just to be an alternative. Boxed lunches that are simple and fast. And if you just want the preserves, that's okay too."

The patrons applauded and Martha circulated with the bread. I was about to clean up the princess mess of pink on my counter, but Milan was quick with a spray bottle.

"I'm going to duck in back and wash the bread pans for another batch," I said to Gran and Katie.

"Let Martha do it," Katie said.

I shook my head. "Let her enjoy the new job. Gran is the star today anyway. Thanks for the help. I'll be back in a few minutes. A little quiet is good too. Did Lurlene leave?" I glanced around.

"I think she went around the time Gran went for lunch." Katie nodded.

"Just checking. Thanks. Let me know if you need me." I patted Gran on the arm.

"It's never been this busy," she said.

"That's your famous bread," I teased.

In the back, I put the bread pans in hot water to soak for a minute and cleaned as I organized, so we wouldn't be slammed tonight.

I put on a beat-up old apron and added soap to the sink just as the noise from the front grew louder. Glancing out, I saw Gus was in the shop.

We hadn't talked much once Hank was under arrest. He'd dropped me at the shop and had a lot of work to do. He'd told me I might be called as a witness to Hank's confession if he retracted it later. I went back to my dishes before he saw me.

A few minutes of blissful scrubbing later and he tapped on the wall.

"Can I come in?" Gus asked.

"Sure. I'm just cleaning up back here. How are things with you, Sheriff?"

"Fine, I just thought I'd update you. Hank did confess fully. He seemed relieved, in a way." Gus hooked his thumbs in the belt loops of his jeans.

"Good. I'm glad." I focused on the pans in front of me and not the attractive man next to me.

"We found his stash of the berries. I guess he kept some extras for his mom, just in case," Gus explained.

"Glad you got the evidence. Oh no, his mother or aunt. She's so sick and he was the only one. Maybe this was temporary insanity for Hank? He was just so stressed?" I wondered aloud.

"You're too nice, Belle. Hopefully he gets a jury that understands the mental strain he was under. It's not our job to convict or dish out the sentence. I contacted the long-term care home and they're aware of the situation with Hank." Gus moved closer. "I want to explain about Dina too."

I shook my head. "I didn't ask. Your past isn't my business."

"I *want* to explain. Dina and I dated for a while, but it didn't work out. We were completely wrong for each other," he said.

"If there's a ring involved, you didn't always think it was *that* wrong. Did you?" I asked.

He sighed. "City life was harder on me. I drank more than I should. There was a case that went bad and things can haunt you. I got to know Dina at the bar and we were off and on. I needed to slow down. Work in a small town, not a big city. I had thought going from Atlanta to Nashville was enough, but it wasn't. I had some rough cases that make Eddie look like preschool. The move was a big change. I'm not blaming anything on her. I ended things suddenly and moved here."

"You told her, right?" I asked.

"Told her what?" he asked.

"It's not my business." I shook my head. "I have work to do."

"I'm still trying to ask you out," Gus said.

I looked at him. Handsome and smart with a job. But also with a past. But it wasn't his parents or family stigma — this was his ex-fiancée.

"I don't think that's a good idea," I replied.

He leaned on the sink. "Because of Dina or your past?"

"I'm not asking you for details on yours, so you don't get details on mine. But if Dina is your type, I'm pretty sure I'm not." I scrubbed like Cinderella — there was no prince coming and I had to make it on my own.

"And I thought you didn't judge," he said.

"I don't. I work in my friend's bar when she needs it. Honest work is nothing to be ashamed of. But if you've given another woman a ring recently enough that she *just* gave it back — I think you need to settle in here longer before you're asking women out. Heal from that relationship and be sure Sweet Grove is where you want to be for the long haul before you start dating anyone. It's not about me or Dina or your past. It's not fair to anyone to use them to get over someone else." I had cleaned the pans in record time with the frustration from the chat.

Gus tapped his hat against his thigh. I tried not to look at him too much. Attraction was hard to ignore, but I didn't want to repeat my mother's mistakes or Dina's. This was my home town and I was staying and not making a mess of my personal life. I didn't need to ruin my reputation…I'd already inherited that much.

"You said it was about your past before. I don't care about my past or yours," he said.

"You should. Small towns are tough. The people are forgiving, but they don't forget. We're close-knit, so if you prove you can't be trusted, everyone will know. If you jilted a fiancée in Nashville, you'll go from the most eligible bachelor to the least. I mean, behind Lou." I chuckled.

Smiling, Gus nodded. "Thanks for the warning. I'd like to tell you the whole story and I want to know yours. You're not ready for that yet. I was hoping we'd get to know each other as we are now first. People change, things change and you're my type."

"But we don't really even know each other yet," I teased.

"You're stubborn," he said.

I rinsed the pans thoroughly. "As a mule, and right now I'm focused on this business succeeding, my Gran being safe and comfortable and helping my friends who are also helping me. Hopefully, no more murders for me to stick my nose into. I promise not to speed."

Gus chuckled softly. "Maybe you're right? Maybe I should settle in and see if Sweet Grove is right for me. See if I win the election before I try to put down real roots."

I set the pans out to dry. "Good plan. Let's get you a coffee."

"I think I'll just go. You've got quite a crowd out there." He left.

I took a deep breath. He was attractive and seemed great, but how many men had tricked women like that? He had a past. Of course we all did, but how much of one? Dina might be one of many for all I knew.

Stepping out front, I discovered that Lurlene and the pastor were now at the counter.

"What's new?" I asked.

Katie turned to me and forced a smile that was a cry for help.

Martha came back with the empty baskets. "People love the bread!"

"Great, how is the stock looking?" I asked.

"Good. Your Gran's guys are keeping an eye. That's a bit odd." Martha blushed

"She's not dating them all. Just friends, I'm pretty sure. Don't think about it. I can't." I waved it off. "Let's try your hazelnut frozen thing."

"Now? That could wait," Martha replied.

"I need the distraction," I said to Martha, who looked over at the counter and shot me a sympathetic nod.

"What can we get for you, Pastor? Lurlene?" Katie asked.

I blended up a hazelnut coffee frozen thing as Martha had suggested. Caramel and mocha I'd already planned but hazelnut was a bit different, not for coffee but the frozen version.

"Berry smoothie," Lurlene said.

"I'll try whatever she's working on now," Pastor Luke said.

I turned. "It's hazelnut. No allergies, right?"

"None. Sounds heavenly," the pastor said.

"Heavenly Hazelnut, there's the name." Katie snapped her fingers and pointed at him.

"As long as it lives up to the pastor's approval." I tasted it quick to be sure it was good. Then I poured him a generous glass full.

Things seemed to quiet down as people waited for the pastor's opinion.

"Truly delicious and heavenly, with or without the coffee," he said.

"Heavenly Hazelnut it is," Gran declared.

"It was all Martha's idea." I poured another and handed it to Martha so she could try it.

"A brilliant idea and a lovely shop. I need to visit with Bea." The pastor slipped from Lurlene's grip and headed to Gran.

Lurlene sipped her smoothie. "Too many seeds."

"You want us to de-seed your strawberries?" Martha asked. "I think she's the real princess."

I stifled a laugh.

Katie grabbed Lurlene's glass and took a sip. "It's perfect. Find something else to complain about. Or find a husband to peel you a bunch of grapes and de-seed your fruit."

I smiled as Lurlene left in a huff.

"One bad seed gone." I sighed.

Katie and Martha laughed.

Maybe Lurlene and Gus deserved each other?

I looked over at the pastor chatting with Gran and her friends. I'd be lying to myself if I said I didn't want romance and true love. I wanted a relationship that worked and was honest. I wasn't there yet. I had some work to do on myself and my business. When I was ready, the right man would be too. He might be here in Sweet Grove already, or he might show up.

"Martha, if you want some bartending shifts after the girls go to bed, you let me know," Katie said.

Strong women didn't tear each other down — they built each other up. I'd made the right friends. Coming home had been tough, but it was the right choice.

"Crap, I have to sign up for that permit to serve alcohol. We should do that class together, Martha. Then we're legit if we need to help Katie," I said.

"Sure. I'll look it up," Martha agreed and consulted with Katie on the website.

Gran waved me over. "You get behind the counter. I want a picture of all my girls."

"Put it on my phone too." I set my phone on the table.

"Pastor, my hands shake. Take a picture of those three, please," Gran said.

"Gran, come on. You have to be in here too." I grabbed her hand.

Gran was in the middle with her arm around me. Katie was on the other side of Gran and, tallest of us, Martha tried to hide behind me with just her head visible. I knew the picture tricks, but whatever made her comfortable.

The camera on my phone flashed a couple of times. Then he used Gran's phone.

"Perfect. That must be printed and go on the wall," the pastor said.

"Thanks, Pastor." I took my phone back and admired the photo.

Pastor Luke stepped in closer. "I wanted to say I was impressed. You managed to stay kind to both Bonnie and Lola in a very uncomfortable position. You helped people without judgment, and that's not easy to do for a lot people."

I wiped my hands on my apron. "Thank you. Everyone has secrets, and finding the truth is complicated."

"You're staying in town then? I heard talk of Atlanta or maybe a job in Nashville?" he asked.

I blushed and looked around. "A friend from Atlanta was interviewing in Nashville. She was just talking about a chance at a job for me if she gets it. Don't count your chickens. And moving to Atlanta is a last resort—I have to be able to take care of Gran."

"You can make it work here." He sounded very confident.

"Well, can't never could, but please put in a good word with the man upstairs." I waved.

"Done. See you for choir practice." He smiled and walked away.

Was he flirting with me? I shook off the praise and flattery that was going to my head. I focused on the picture and all the work ahead of me.

No doubt about it, I was home.

A Note from Belle

Hey y'all,

I can't believe the drama. A murder in Sweet Grove. Never happens here. It can't possibly happen again, right?

And Gus…just what we need. A tempting guy with a past. I have enough skeletons in my family's closet. I'm not sure if I'm voting for him or against him…but I've got time to decide.

Well, I hope you come back and visit us again. New things on the menu and new friends to meet. I'll keep Lurlene away from you, I promise!

And no more murders! It's Sweet Grove, for heaven's sake!

Appreciate cha!

Belle

Want to see more like this?
Here's a taster for you to enjoy!

Manitoba Tea & Tarot Mysteries:
Magic, Mayhem & Murder
January Bain

Excerpt

*The most beautiful thing we can experience is the mysterious.
It is the source of all true art and science. — Albert Einstein*

Thirteen years ago

"Will she let us stay?" Tulip's eyes widened, her nose and cheeks reddened by the freezing wind. My triplet shivered, wiping her dripping nose on the back of her red mitten. I straightened the collar on her worn jacket and tucked the thin scarf around her neck. The snow was falling more heavily now, already filling in the tracks the three of us had made walking from the street light to the front stoop, the warning still ringing in my head. *'Don't knock until you've counted to a hundred if you know what's good for you.'* Twelve, thirteen, fourteen...

"I'm not sure, but if we're really, really good, she might. At least for tonight," I interrupted my counting to answer her.

"Yeah, don't you be backtalking her like you did to Mommy," Star said, staring accusingly.

"I never did that!" Tulip's bottom lip started to quiver.

"Hush, no one is at fault," I said. If she started bawling, I didn't know how long I could hold off. My throat had a lump in it big as a baseball. *Thirty-one, thirty-two, thirty-three.*

Star screwed up her face but held her tongue, though only after I gave her my sternest older-sister look. I'd been born at one minute to midnight, making me the oldest sister by a full day. Not that birthdays were ever celebrated, though we'd had eight already. Mommy said we were too much trouble on a regular day. No way was she holding a two-day party for a trio of brats.

I tugged the paper sack holding all our possessions closer to my chest, thinking of the one precious book and the half-box of Pop-Tarts Mommy had tucked inside for our supper. Maybe Granny would have a toaster or a stove element to warm them up? Or maybe she might have some juice or pop? My throat was dry. Even water would taste good.

Star stamped her feet to stay warm, her pink running shoes leaving an intricate pattern from the soles as she packed the snow. Her scarf had icicles forming from her warm breath hitting the frosty air and her cheeks shone bright red. No frostbite—not yet anyway. But the wind was picking up, blowing showers of ice crystals off the roof and onto our bare heads.

Sixty-six, sixty-seven. I glanced across the open field between Granny's house and the house next door, visualizing wolves coming out of the evergreens of the thick forest and circling the town. We'd been dropped off on one of the coldest days of the year. Minus forty-seven, according to the loud man on the radio in our old van. I'd caught the name of the town on the welcoming sign leading in. *Snowy Lake, population 1259.* I was proud to be the first one to learn to read, first one to do most things. Then I could help my little sisters, when they'd let me.

Eighty-nine, ninety. I was shaking now, could barely keep from kicking at the door with my foot. But a promise is a promise. If Mommy came back and saw me doing wrong, I'd get a swat for sure. *You know she's not coming back, right?* a small voice inside me piped up, making tears well. *No! Don't ever say that.* Hard as times had been, Mommy loved us deep down inside. *She's coming back. One day.* When things were better for her, she'd be back. She promised. And if I kept my solemn promise to look after my sisters, then everything would be okay. It had to be.

"Okay, let's not forget who we are. The awesome McCalls. Okay, time's up."

Just as I reached one hundred the back-porch light came on, a beacon in the darkness, spotlighting the three of us huddled in the dark.

"Land's sake alive, what are the three of you doing outside waiting in the snow?"

I spoke up, holding out the bedraggled piece of paper with the slightly smeared ink. "Granny Toogood, my mommy said to give you this."

If she was surprised at me calling her Granny, she didn't show it. She took the offering and read it with an intense expression. I peeked at her while she read. Dark curls gleamed around a soft face. She was wearing a nice pair of blue slacks with a matching blouse over a slim body, no stains or holes. *She must be rich.* She was shorter than Mommy, too. When she glanced down at Star, Tulip and me, the expression in her blue eyes was kind, as though she was very sure of something. I liked her immediately. I badly wanted her to like me, too. Then maybe she would feel obliged to help my sisters.

"Well, let's get you all inside then," she said, refolding and tucking the letter into her pants pocket.

I waited until my sisters had clamored in the doorway before I glanced back at the forest. The pack of wolves had vanished.

Home of Erotic Romance

Sign up for our newsletter and find out about all our romance book releases, eBook sales and promotions, sneak peeks and FREE romance books!

About the Author

A loyal Chicago girl who loves deep dish pizza, the Cubs, and The Lake, her close fam moved to TN so she ends up visiting the South more than she ever planned! CC Dragon is fascinated by the magical and paranormal as well as the quirks of the south. She loves creating characters who solve mysteries. A coffee and chocolate addict who loves fast cars, she's still looking for a hero who likes to cook and clean…so she can write more!

CC Dragon loves to hear from readers. You can find her contact information, website details and author profile page at https://www.totallybound.com